GRAVEYARD
Promises

Graveyard Promises

Kathleen Kelly

Disclaimer: The material in this book contains graphic language and sexual content and is intended for mature audiences, ages 18 and older.

ISBN: 978-1-922883-20-9

Editing by Swish Design & Editing
Proofreading by Swish Design & Editing
Book design by Swish Design & Editing
Cover design by CT Cover Creations
Cover Image Copyright 2025
First Edition 2025

DEDICATION

To the authors, bloggers, and readers
who share my work.
It is more appreciated than you know.
Happy Halloween!

PROLOGUE

Sophia Chavez
Halloween 2024

Halloween night is my favorite night of the year. The air hums with mischief and possibility, the faint tang of smoke from jack-o'-lanterns curls around the manicured gardens of our estate.

Papa's parties are legendary—so many faces, so much glittering wealth, laughter echoing through the halls—it's the perfect cover for slipping away unnoticed. I do just that, ducking out once his speech is finished and he's paraded his latest female prize like a trophy.

Mother died a year after I was born, leaving

Papa with three sons and me, his little princess, wrapped in silk and shields. I'm twenty-two now, a woman of my own mind, but the rules are clear—I am to stay ignorant of the family business. Of course, it doesn't take a genius to see the truth. Papa and my brothers control one of the most powerful cartels in the country, their names whispered in fear as easily as they are praised in society.

My role is simple—earn a university degree, marry a wealthy, connected man, bear grandchildren, and never step foot into the world I truly crave. The world of art. I adore it. Painting, sketching, and sculpting are the only places where I can be myself, free from Papa's shadows. I had dreamed of Paris, wandering the galleries along the Seine, absorbing centuries of beauty, and living a life that belonged to *me*. But Papa's answer was always the same, *"Stay here, my princess, your life is already chosen."*

This year was different. I finished my bachelor's degree a year early, my final project piece a statement of defiance and devotion. And tonight, I can taste the possibility of freedom in the crisp fall air.

I slip through the throng of guests, heels clicking softly against the marble floors, my painted face a mask of color and bone instead of leather or velvet masks. The Day of the Dead makeup smudges slightly under my lashes, but I don't care. Papa appreciated the effort I went to in using my skills to cover my identity, but was disappointed he could not show off his beautiful daughter.

The gardens are quiet once I reach them, the warm chatter of the party fading behind me. Flickering lanterns hang from the trees, casting skeletal shadows across the hedges. I breathe deep, tasting the brisk air tinged with the sweet decay of fallen leaves, and for the first time tonight, I feel untethered.

Free.

My friend, Maria, is waiting on the other side of our estate, crouched in the shadows in her car. I slip through the fence and tap on her window, scaring her half to death.

"Sophia! Geez! I thought your father was here to teach me a lesson."

Laughing, I move around the car and slide in. "Sorry. He has no idea. Calm down."

"*You* calm down. You're not the one who's going to be wearing cement shoes if anything happens to you." Maria tilts her head and eyes my costume. "Side note, you look hot. How did your papa feel about your boobs being on display?"

"He didn't notice the costume, only that my face was covered."

We laugh. Maria knows how protective my father and brothers are because they practically suffocate me.

She puts the car in drive, and we leave my family and their secrets behind.

"Where are we going?" I ask.

Maria raises her eyebrows and grins. "Only the best party in Miami."

"You say that every year."

"Girl, that's because I *take* you to the best parties every year."

"Where's your costume?"

"In the back. I can't drive with it on. You're going to love it."

Maria is five feet tall with long, dark curly hair and the biggest brown eyes, but her Halloween costumes are always *weird*. One year, she went as a pumpkin, another year as *Beetlejuice*. She never shows off her curves or how pretty she is.

Downtown Miami comes alive outside the windshield, neon reflecting off the wet streets, the hum of traffic blending with distant music. Maria suddenly throws the car into reverse and parks.

"Ha! Got ourselves a good park. We won't have far to walk."

"That's good. Maybe my whiplash will appreciate the shorter distance," I say, laughing.

"Pfft!" Maria waves me off and jumps out of the car. She digs into the trunk and pulls out a huge, bright orange Halloween basket with a handle. Then she steps inside, hoists it up her body, and clips it to her black shorts so it won't fall.

"You're a candy bucket?"

"Yep."

"You recycled the pumpkin, didn't you?"

"Hey, I upcycled. Not all of us can afford an expensive costume."

Pointing at my corset and long skirt, I say, "This is from my wardrobe. And I did the makeup myself."

"It looks amazing."

"Come on, let's go find the party of the year."

Maria bounces in place. "I got us invites." She slams the trunk and does a drumroll. "Obsidian."

"How did you score that?"

"My crappy brother isn't so crappy after all. He's working there and got us tickets."

"When did Vincent get that job?"

"He goes by 'V' now. Been there a couple of months. Be nice, or he won't let us in."

I salute, and we link arms, which is awkward because of Maria's size, and end up laughing and holding hands as we approach the club's entrance.

V is standing at his post, and his face falls when he sees his sister. Maria twirls at the bottom of the stairs, then struts up to him.

"Jesus, Maria, can't you ever wear something *cool*?" He shakes his head. "Why can't you be more like Sophia?"

"She'd be boring if she were more like me," I defend her.

"Yeah, but she'd look better," V counters.

With a sigh, he unclips the black velvet rope and gestures for us to go inside. We kiss him on the cheek as the line of people waiting groans.

Maria turns, holding the tickets high. "We've

got tickets, biatches."

V's eyes widen, and I giggle, shoving my friend into the club.

The bass hits me the moment we step inside, vibrating through the marble floors and up into my chest. Obsidian is everything Maria promised—dark, sleek, and dripping with neon. Shadows swirl over velvet-draped walls, red and purple lights cutting across faces hidden behind ornate masks. A fog machine drifts lazily over the crowd, curling around heels and cocktail glasses alike.

I inhale, catching the scent of expensive perfume, smoke, and something a little metallic underneath. My pulse quickens, not just from the music, but from the thrill of being somewhere forbidden, somewhere Papa and his men can't touch me. Not tonight. Tonight, I belong only to myself and the shadows.

Maria yanks me toward the bar, where people in elaborate costumes laugh and drink, their voices mixing with the deep hum of music. I notice the attention my face draws. The Day of the Dead makeup is striking under colored lighting, my painted skull grinning at anyone daring enough to stare. I smirk to myself—*Papa may not have wanted my face hidden, but this way, everyone sees me, and no one knows me. Perfect.*

"Drink?" Maria leans close, her lips brushing my ear, and I feel the tickle of her laugh vibrating against my skin.

"Something strong," I reply, glancing around. My eyes land on a corner of the room where the crowd thins slightly, shadows pooling against the black walls.

Maria hands me my drink and then prances toward the dance floor like a little whirlwind in her upcycled pumpkin costume. I follow reluctantly, letting the rhythm of the music pull me in, allowing the mask on my face and the anonymity of the crowd to make me bold.

And then I see *him*.

Tall, broad, the kind of man who doesn't just enter a room, he *claims* it. Dark hair, leather jacket, a mask obscuring his eyes, but I feel the intensity of his gaze as if it's drilling straight through me.

He doesn't look at anyone else.

Not the laughing girls.

Not the people drinking too loudly.

Not even the bouncers at the door.

Only me.

I freeze mid-step, my heartbeat stuttering. Something deep in my gut twists, a dangerous curiosity I can't resist. I'm not supposed to notice him. I'm not supposed to feel anything. But the pull is there, electric and undeniable.

"Move it, Sophia!" Maria tugs me forward, laughing, but I can't tear my eyes away.

The man shifts slightly, and my breath catches. I know I should look away. I *want* to look away. But I don't.

And then, in one fluid motion, he steps toward me, weaving through the crowd as if everyone else is frozen. His presence commands the room, and when he stops just a foot away, I see a glimmer of something behind the mask—danger, amusement, and something... magnetic.

"Do I know you?" My voice is louder than I meant it to be, cutting through the music, my skull-painted grin daring him.

He tilts his head, a slow, teasing gesture, the mask hiding the rest. No answer, just a glance that tells me he's already decided something, and

I have no idea what.

And in that moment, Halloween becomes more than a night of costumes. It becomes a night of sparks, danger, and a temptation I can't name... *yet*.

The crowd swirls around us, bodies moving in rhythm to the pounding beat, but it feels like we're in our own bubble. His presence presses close, a warmth I didn't expect, and I suddenly notice the way the mask doesn't hide the sharp intelligence in his eyes.

"Can I buy you a drink?" he asks finally, his voice low, just above the music.

I raise an eyebrow and hold up my glass. "I've got one."

He nods. "How about we get out of here?"

"Do I look like the type to fall for masked strangers?"

A slow smile spreads beneath the mask. "Maybe not, but maybe the type to break the rules."

I laugh a little breathlessly and step closer. My heels glide against the floor as I follow him into the moving crowd, letting the rhythm guide us. He's close enough that I can feel the heat radiating off him, a dangerous, sexy energy that makes the back of my neck tingle.

"What's your name?" I ask, keeping my tone casual, though my heart is doing that stupid fluttering thing that never stops when danger and attraction collide.

He shakes his head, the movement deliberate, teasing. "Names are overrated. Tonight... I just need to know you're paying attention."

I smirk, daring him further. "I am. You're... *interesting*, I'll give you that. But I'm not leaving here with you. You could be dangerous."

"Dangerous is exactly why I approached you," he says, and I catch the faintest edge of amusement in his voice. "And I can tell you don't scare easily."

Tilting my head, I pretend not to notice the way my pulse jumps. "I've had practice."

He leans just a fraction closer, enough that I feel the brush of his sleeve against mine. "Good. Then maybe you'll enjoy the night ahead."

I shiver, and it's impossible to tell whether it's the air, the music, or the way he watches me like he's sizing me up. The thrill of unknown danger, of someone who could be anywhere from charming to deadly, sends a shiver down my spine.

And just like that, the night shifts. The masks, the costumes, the glittering chaos are background now. He's the only thing that matters, a spark I can't quite touch, and somehow, I know I shouldn't.

Yet I can't look away.

He takes my hand before I can protest, and I feel the weight of his gaze like a physical touch. The music pulses through the floor, reverberating in my chest, and suddenly we're moving together, slipping into the rhythm as if the world outside this club doesn't exist.

His hands are careful at first—one on my waist, the other brushing against my back—but there's an unmistakable edge of exploration, like he's testing boundaries, learning what's new to him. I can't help the sharp intake of breath that escapes me when his fingers graze my hip, light but deliberate, sending heat curling through me like I've never known.

Without meaning to, I stiffen slightly, unsure of how to respond. I've been sheltered my whole life, wrapped in silk and shields, my body mostly mine but my heart... often watched, often controlled. Now, pressed against him, I feel something else entirely—curiosity, longing, and yes, a hint of fear that excites me in ways I shouldn't admit.

"You're tense," he murmurs against my ear, his voice low and teasing. "Relax. Feel it. Let it guide you."

Swallowing hard, I nod, forcing a small laugh, though my pulse is thrumming in my throat. "I-I don't... I'm not used to this."

A chuckle rumbles from him, deep and amused, and I feel the vibration along my shoulder. "Not used to being wanted?"

The bluntness of the question makes my stomach flip, and I shake my head, cheeks warming beneath the paint. "I've... never danced this close."

"Hmm," he hums, his hand sliding slightly higher on my back, pressing closer, testing me without rushing. "Then tonight, you're allowed to explore. No rules. Just you and me."

It's ridiculous.

Dangerous and thrilling.

My hand drifts to his chest almost without

thinking, feeling the solid heat of him beneath the fabric, the pulse of hard muscle. I'm learning, inch by inch, the rhythm of closeness, the way my body reacts to his touch, and the feel of him pressed against me.

His other hand finds mine, lacing our fingers together, firm and possessive, guiding my movements. Every brush of his palm, every shift of his body against mine, feels like it's writing a secret language I didn't know I wanted to learn.

"Relax your shoulders," he whispers, and I do, letting him take over the sway, the lift, the turn. His body is confident, skilled, and I am raw, unpracticed, every nerve alight with sensation. I can't stop the shiver that travels up my spine when his hand glides along my side, daring but patient, as though he knows exactly how far he can push.

Closing my eyes for a moment, I let the music and his touch guide me. This is forbidden, intoxicating, and utterly new. And somehow, I'm not scared. Not yet.

"Good girl," he murmurs near my ear, the words grazing my skin like fire. "You're... perfect tonight."

And just like that, the world narrows to his hands, the rhythm, the heat, the spark of something I've never been allowed to feel.

"Princess, you ignoring me over here?" Maria's voice slices through the club like a flare, full of mock outrage. She's only a few feet away, hands on her hips, eyes sparkling with mischief.

I bite back a laugh, and for a moment, the intimacy of his touch feels almost... *wrong.* Almost. I give him a small, apologetic smile, the one that says *this isn't over*, and step back, letting his hands fall away.

Maria's grin widens as I slip to her side. "There she is. I thought you were going to leave me lonely out here, huh?"

"I'm here," I say, laughing, and she pulls me into a spin. The candy-bucket costume flares around her, bright and ridiculous, and I can't help but smile, feeling the ease of her friendship like a lifeline.

"You're glowing tonight, Princess," Maria teases, leaning in so only I can hear. "But you're making the poor masked stranger over there sweat bullets."

I glance over my shoulder, and yes, he's still

watching, his mask angled slightly, the tilt of his head and the way his eyes narrow making my pulse skip. My stomach flutters with a delicious mix of thrill and nerves.

Maria tugs me toward the bar. "Come on, Princess, let's get another drink before you melt on me."

Snorting, I say, "I don't need to be handled. I just... I can't help myself."

She laughs and loops her arm through mine. "Then don't. Just have fun. Tonight, nothing else matters."

And I do. I let myself fall into the chaos of the club, the laughter, the music, the freedom of being with Maria. But even in the midst of the fun, even with my mask-smudged smile and candy-bucket friend beside me, I can't stop the pull toward him.

I know before this night is over, I'll find him again.

The clock in my mind screams almost one, and

reality crashes in—I have to get home before someone notices I'm missing. Maria, oblivious as always, is still laughing and waving her hands to the music. Grabbing her hand, I weave us through the crowd to the club's entrance. The cool night air outside hits me like a breath of freedom, brisk and tingling against my flushed skin.

Maria spins toward me, grin wide, but freezes mid-step. Her dark eyes flick to the street. "Uh-oh," she murmurs.

V stands there, jaw tight, eyes narrowing like only a disapproving older brother can. "Maria," he says, not a greeting, just her name, low and serious. "We need to talk."

I glance at Maria, who shoots me a quick, conspiratorial shrug. She's used to this. I nod, letting her lead the way a few steps ahead. "Go on," she murmurs. "I'll catch up."

Maria flashes me a reassuring smile, then turns to face her brother. I slip past them, heading down the stairs toward her car.

I'm nearly at the car when a hand clamps over my wrist. My breath catches. I'm spun back against a wall, chest pressing into a solid, impossibly firm body. The masked stranger from the club looms close, hands bracketing me against the brick. My heart stutters as fear swirls with something far more dangerous.

"Princess," he murmurs, low and teasing, the mask hiding his expression but not the intent in his voice. "Where do you think you're going?"

"I... I'm just—" I falter, my voice thin. My inexperience with men, with this, with *him*, tangles with the thrill surging through me.

His hands move, tracing lightly along my arms, sending shivers I can't control through my body. He doesn't rush, doesn't demand, and I want to run, but the warmth and strength of him keep me pinned, caught somewhere between fear and longing.

"You shouldn't disappear," he whispers, his breath brushing my ear. One hand slides up, fingers lingering near my neck, close enough to feel the heat radiating from him. "Not when I've been waiting all night."

I press my palms against his chest, tiny against the solid muscle beneath his shirt. "I-I'm not... I'm not..." *Experienced, sheltered, unprepared.* Words fail me.

A soft chuckle rumbles from him, vibrating

through the wall behind us. "Not used to being wanted?" His fingers trace slowly along my jawline, teasing me.

My knees threaten to buckle. My pulse hammers in my ears. "I-I don't know what you mean," I whisper, voice barely audible.

He tilts his head, masking a smile I can feel more than see. "Then let me show you," he murmurs, leaning closer, and the scent of him, warm, dangerous, and intoxicating, fills my senses.

I try to swallow, to steady my racing heart, but my body betrays me, arching slightly into his touch, responding to every brush of his hands, every inch of heat pressing into mine. My mind screams caution, yet something inside me trembles with reckless curiosity.

He leans just slightly closer, eyes locked on mine, voice dropping to a near growl. "Princess, don't look away from me. Not now."

Biting my lip, I'm torn between warning myself to flee and the raw, thrilling pull that won't let me.

He leans closer, my pulse is deafening, my breath shallow, and I know he can feel it through the brush of his body against mine.

Then, he closes the distance. His lips touch mine, softly at first, a whisper that makes my knees weaken and my stomach flip. I freeze, unsure what to do, my hands clutching at his chest, heart pounding against my ribs.

"Princess..." His voice is rough, low, and the way he says my nickname sends shivers straight through me.

His mouth presses harder, confident, insistent, and I finally respond, not fully, not with skill, but with curiosity and instinct. My lips part, and his tongue traces mine gently, exploring, coaxing, and I gasp at the sensation, overwhelmed by how foreign and... *thrilling* it feels.

My hands fumble against him, inexperienced and shaky, brushing along the planes of his chest, feeling the taut muscle beneath my fingers. His hands roam carefully, possessively, along my arms, my waist, sliding over the curve of my back, keeping me close.

It's dizzying, intoxicating with every nerve alight, every breath stolen. I should pull away, I *know* I should, but the pull is magnetic, and I melt into the kiss despite my better judgment.

He tilts my head gently, deepening the kiss just

enough to make my knees threaten to buckle entirely. My hands clutch at his shoulders, fingers digging in, heart racing like a drum in my chest.

Finally, he breaks away, just enough to let me breathe, his forehead resting against mine, his lips still brushing mine with every heartbeat. His eyes, dark and unreadable behind the mask, hold me captive.

"Princess..." he murmurs again, teasing, dangerous, so certain of himself. "You're... different. Fragile and fierce at the same time. And I want all of it."

My chest heaves, my lips tingle from his touch, and I realize how much I've craved this, craved *him*, even if I didn't know it until this very moment.

A noise from the street snaps me slightly back to reality—the distant hum of traffic, the faint echo of music from the club—but the heat between us refuses to dissipate. I pull back a fraction, breathless, heart thundering, and he lets me, just holding me there, pressed against him, a tether I'm not ready to break.

"Stay with me," he whispers, voice low and rough. "Just a little longer."

And against every warning, every lesson from a lifetime of being watched and protected, I nod because I *want* to.

Before I can melt entirely into him, a familiar, sharp voice cuts through the alley, "Princess! Where are you?"

Maria's waving frantically from the end of the alley, her grin bright and teasing. My stomach drops. *Oh no, she's found me.* Slowly, I pull back from this man, brushing my hands lightly against his chest, taking a breath to steady myself.

He watches me, every inch of him tense, his gaze dark and unreadable behind the mask. My lips still tingle from the kiss, my body humming with the memory, but I can't—*no, I shouldn't*—stay here.

"I-I have to go," I stammer, a smile tugging at the corners of my lips, more for Maria than him.

Maria bounds toward me, looping her arm through mine. "Sorry to break up the party, but we need to get you home before you turn into a pumpkin."

His hand hovers for a heartbeat, like he wants to stop me, to pull me back, but he doesn't.

Raphael leans slightly closer, his voice low and dangerous. "Be careful, Princess," he murmurs, letting the words linger like smoke. "This night doesn't have to be over."

I glance back at him once, catching the intensity in his gaze, feeling it burn straight through me. Then I force my attention back to Maria, trying to shake the dizzy warmth still clinging to my skin.

"Come on," Maria says, tugging me along. "Let's get some air before your papa sends a search party."

As we step farther down the street, the club's music fades behind us. Maria chatters on about some ridiculous costume mishap, and her laughter is loud and infectious. I laugh along, but one eye never leaves the alley where he lingers, leaning casually against the wall.

Maria bumps my shoulder playfully. "Hey, Princess, you're all quiet. Did we have a little Halloween adventure?"

I smile, shaking my head. "Yeah, I did."

She winks. "Don't forget... we've got more fun to get into. And tonight isn't over yet. Your family's party will still be going strong."

A sudden movement catches my attention, and my heart skips. Raphael steps closer, the dim streetlight flickering across his mask. He reaches out, brushing a loose strand of hair from my face. "Princess..." His voice is low, intimate. "I need to know your name. And... maybe, could I get your number?"

Heat blooms in my chest, and my pulse quickens. Every instinct in me is drawn to him, but Maria's sharp elbow in my side snaps me out of my daze.

"Uh-uh, Princess," Maria hisses, grabbing my hand and pulling me slightly back. "No names, no numbers. Not tonight."

I glance at her, confused, but Maria's expression is firm.

Raphael frowns, tilting his head, mask shadowing his face. "I understand..." His tone is almost disappointed, but there's a promise hidden in it, something that makes my stomach twist in anticipation. "Another night, then?"

I can't help the small, mischievous smile that slips across my lips. "Maybe—" I murmur before Maria tugs me farther down the street, cutting me off before I can say more.

"Come on, Princess," Maria says again, her voice teasing but insistent. "Let's leave Mr. Mysterious to his shadows and enjoy the rest of our night."

I glance over my shoulder one last time, catching the way he watches me, the dark promise in his stance, and I shiver. It's not from the cool air but from something far hotter.

As Maria pulls me toward the car, laughter and music surrounding us, I know one thing for certain...

This Halloween has been my best yet.

CHAPTER *One*

Raphael 'The Reaper' Costa
Halloween 2025

Halloween night wraps the Chavez estate in a cloak of shadows and flickering light. Lanterns hang from the oaks along the water's edge, their carved faces grinning like silent witnesses to the night's mischief. Fog drifts across the manicured lawns, curling around marble fountains, carrying the scent of the ocean mingled with pumpkin spice and cigar smoke. Music and laughter spill from the grand house, but beneath the gaiety, the air hums with unspoken tension.

This night, there's a gathering of wealth,

influence, and veiled threats. The Chavez and Costa families, longtime enemies in a war that has stretched across generations, each tried to claim Miami and other cities as their own.

Everyone here knows the rules...

Be polite, smile, enter into conversations but say nothing to embarrass the family, and keep plenty of distance or risk a confrontation that would make the headlines by morning.

I am Raphael 'The Reaper' Costa, and I dislike being on enemy territory. Standing on the fringe, I am a predator in human form—tall, lethal, and measured. My mask conceals the scarred perfection of my face. I do *not* mingle. I survey the house, the grounds, the guests, every detail before stepping into the lion's den.

And then I see *her.*

Sophia, Hector Chavez's daughter, who is floating through the crowd in a gown of deep crimson, her dark hair swept up into a sparkling crown. Lanterns catch it as she turns, the light bouncing off the jewels, illuminating the curve of her smile as she greets the people around her. She's twenty-three, educated, refined, and every bit the princess her costume suggests. Spoiled, probably boring, living under her father's watchful eye on this well-guarded estate.

And yet, I can't take my eyes off her.

Because my mind refuses to categorize her as ordinary.

I let my eyes trace the line of her neck, the curve of her shoulders beneath the crimson fabric, the subtle tension in her posture. She's aware of the room, of her father's proximity, and on the surface, she appears to be the perfect woman Hector Chavez shows off to the world.

A woman dressed as Ursula sidles up to her, linking her arm with Sophia's. She looks familiar, the way they laugh at something I can't hear. There's something about them—an energy I can't quite place, a spark I can't ignore.

"Yo, bro, Dad wants you." My younger brother, Gabriel, nudges me with his elbow.

"The woman next to Sophia Chavez... who is she?"

Gabriel shrugs. "No idea. Want me to find out?"

"Yes."

"You like her?"

"No." I glance at him. "Remember the woman from last year?"

"You mean the one you obsessed over for three months?"

"Not that long." In truth, it's been the entire year, but I don't need my brother teasing me, not here, not tonight. "Where's Dad?"

He points across the crowd. My father raises a hand, standing with a group of Chavez men. I wave back and, without looking at Gabriel, say, "Find out who Ursula is."

"V might know. He's here tonight."

Pausing, I turn to study him. "Why is he here? Did he come with us?"

"No, he told Frank he's known Sophia forever. Apparently, his sister and Sophia are best friends."

It hits me then. *Ursula, the friend from last Halloween.* Could Sophia Chavez be my princess? Surely not.

"You'd better go. Dad's looking annoyed."

Nodding, I cast Sophia Chavez a quick glance. My pulse quickens, and a low, familiar heat coils in my chest. *It could be her.*

I push my thoughts of her aside, just for a moment, and head toward my father. He's across the lawn, flanked by a group of Chavez men who look every bit as tense as the atmosphere itself. Everyone here knows the rules, knows the stakes, and one wrong move could undo a year of careful planning.

"Father," I say, keeping my tone measured, formal.

My father's eyes narrow beneath the brim of his hat, scanning me like he's reading for weakness.

"Raphael," he acknowledges with a curt nod, his voice low, controlled. "Enjoying yourself? This is Antonio Chavez, the eldest son of Hector. Antonio, this is my oldest son, Raphael."

Antonio holds out his hand. "The Reaper?"

"Raphael is fine." I give a tight smile.

"Your work precedes you," replies Antonio.

"As does yours."

"Gentlemen, we aren't here to fight but to find common ground. You two will one day rule, so it's important we get along," my father states.

Dad pats us both on the back and walks toward Hector Chavez. I look pointedly at one of our men. He taps another, and they flank him but stay a few steps back.

"Paranoid?" asks Antonio.

"Not at all. I've found it pays to be careful."

I glance at the Chavez men standing close, posture rigid, hands just shy of the weapons hidden beneath their coats. They're watching me as closely as I watch them. Tension crackles in the air like static before a storm.

"Does your family do this often?" I ask Antonio.

"This is Papa's biggest party all year. Christmas is a less formal affair, family only."

"Everyone who's anyone is here. Looks like a success," I add.

Antonio makes a sucking sound, hands in his pockets, and nods toward our fathers. "I guess that remains to be seen. Enjoy your night."

I tilt my head slightly. "I will."

The conversation is brief, but enough to remind me why this gathering is a dangerous game. I pivot, taking a slow path through the crowd, eyes scanning, calculating.

And then I see her. She's not in a crowd, just beyond the fountains, standing with Ursula. Crimson against the cold marble, her head tilts slightly as she laughs with her friend. My breath catches. My pulse hammers.

I move carefully, deliberately, keeping the

crowd between us as cover. Every step is measured, every inch a balance between not drawing attention and closing the distance. My hands tighten briefly on the lapels of my jacket. She doesn't know it yet, but I see her. I *know* her.

As I get closer, I notice the subtle details—the way her fingers curl around Ursula's arm, the light catching the edges of her mask, the tension in her shoulders as if she's aware of every movement around her. I remember last year, the reckless defiance beneath a carefully guarded exterior.

Tonight, I will find out if she's the same girl who haunted me for twelve months.

Weaving through the clusters of guests, being careful to appear casual, but every sense is sharpened. Music pulses through the air, laughter and chatter a mask for the watchful eyes beneath ornate costumes. Men in tailored suits and masks of gold and black glance my way. I nod, polite, formal, but I am not here for them. I am here for *her*.

Crimson. My eyes find that color again and again, cutting through the throng, like a thread pulling me closer. Ursula drifts alongside her, laughing, their hands brushing occasionally, fingers curling together in familiarity. I notice every detail, the tilt of her chin, the way the mask obscures the smile in her eyes, but cannot hide the curve of her lips. The subtle twitch of her shoulder tells me she feels eyes on her. I do. I *always* have.

I pause at a fountain, pretending to adjust my cuff, letting her drift a few steps ahead. My pulse slows only fractionally as I study her from afar, calculating my approach. She isn't looking for me. She doesn't know who I am.

I move again, careful to follow the natural flow of the crowd, letting it act as cover. A group of Chavez men passes between us, and I pause, letting them block the view for a heartbeat longer than necessary. Her laugh echoes, a light, musical sound that claws at me, familiar and teasing.

I remind myself... *Not yet. Patience.*

The distance closes slowly, inches at a time. A waiter passes with a tray of champagne flutes, and I step into the shadow of his path, merging with the crowd as if by accident. My hands remain in my jacket pockets, casual and controlled, but my mind calculates every potential risk.

She tilts her head, catching the light in her mask, and something in me stirs. I've had haunted nights with the memory of her last Halloween, her voice, the curve of her lips beneath that small, perfect grin. *Could it be her? Could the girl who tormented my thoughts for a year really be here, right in front of me, laughing like she belongs?*

Maria—Princess's shadow—nudges her slightly, gaining her attention. The moment is perfect. I step closer, letting the crowd's chatter shield me from prying eyes. One more turn around the fountain, one more careful weave between groups, and I am within arm's reach.

I stop just outside the small circle of light bathing her face, my presence a whisper in the chaos. Ursula glances toward me, curiosity flickering in her gaze, but she doesn't speak. Sophia does not see me yet, or maybe she does, she appears good at hiding things.

My eyes roam over her, drinking her in. Every movement, every gesture, every heartbeat in the rhythm of her stance pulls me forward. And then...

She turns her head slightly, as if sensing something, and our eyes meet beneath the masks.

Recognition? Maybe.

Intrigue? Definitely.

Desire? Undeniable.

The air between us ignites. It's silent, electric, and oh so dangerous.

Taking another step, I close the distance, careful not to startle her.

My voice drops low, almost a murmur beneath the hum of the party. "Enjoying the night?"

Her mask tilts, a hint of amusement in the curve of her lips. "And who wants to know?"

The game has begun.

CHAPTER
Two

Sophia

He's tall, dark, and undeniably handsome. But there's something familiar about him—the curve of his smile, the way his eyes crinkle just enough to wish the mask weren't hiding them. I shouldn't even be noticing, not at Papa's party, not with the sea of strangers I don't know or don't want to know.

Maybe he's different.

"I like your costume."

I twirl, letting my laughter float in the air. "My father picked it."

He glances past me at Maria. "And your

costumes never disappoint. That candy bucket from last year, reinvented?"

I tilt my head, stepping back, pretending to examine Maria while catching the glint in his eyes. She's completely oblivious to his dig about last year, and how does he know?

"Hey, some of us have to work with what we've got," Maria says with a shrug. "Although... this is probably the last year I can get away with revamping this one. Three years in a row, and after not being able to clean it properly, it's ready for the scrap heap."

She looks up at me and smiles, but like the good friend she is, she senses something is off.

I reach for her hand for support, my pulse quickening, and ask him, "How... how did you know Maria was a candy bucket last year?"

He scans the crowd, then tilts his head toward me. "I preferred your costume last year too. Your take on *Día de los Muertos*... much more suited than this outfit, Princess."

My hand flutters to my chest.

Maria laughs, eyes sparkling. "It's *you*! The sexy stranger from last year at the club."

"Maria! Lower your voice. And remember,

Papa has ears everywhere."

Frantically, I scan the crowd, my chest tightening with every moving body. Someone could be watching, someone could be *listening*.

He reaches out, his fingers curling around mine. My pulse stutters at the contact.

"No one is close. You're safe," he murmurs, his voice low, teasing... almost intimate.

A tingle shoots from my hand straight to my heart. I jerk it back, heat blooming in my chest. "We should... we should be going."

He leans just a fraction closer, and I smell the faint trace of him—something warm, sharp, and dangerous. "The night is young. I was hoping we could pick up where we left off last year, Sophia."

I take another careful step back, trying to create distance, but my legs feel too short, my body betraying me.

"You're on my father's territory. He's brokering some kind of deal tonight, and trust me, you *do not* want to be on his bad side by flirting with his only daughter."

His grin flickers, eyes glinting with mischief. "Flirting, huh? That's a shame because I think you did more than flirt with me last year."

My breath catches. I want to look away, to hide the heat crawling up my neck, but I *can't*.

"Raphael, you're wanted inside," Gabriel calls, striding toward us.

"Can it wait?" I ask, trying to sound casual.

He grins, sharp and knowing. "Nope. Dad's in the office of our host... and it looks heated."

"*Fuck*," he mutters, then glances at me. "I'll be back."

"Raphael '*The Reaper*' Costa?" My voice comes out sharper than I intend, and a little startled.

"Just Raphael," he says, tilting his head, eyes flicking over me like he's memorizing every detail.

"But you're not. You're the enforcer for the Costa family." I grab Maria's hand, tugging her back. "You're not someone I want to know."

He chuckles, low and amused, with a dangerous glint in his eyes. "But, Princess... you already do."

A shiver runs down my spine. That wink—like he knows exactly what he's doing—makes me want to glance away, but I can't. My pulse kicks up, hot and frantic, and I know I'm far more aware of him than I should be.

With a final smirk, he turns, his brother trailing behind, and disappears into my home, leaving a trail of heat and questions I didn't ask.

"Holy shit, he's cute."

"No, he's not. He's dangerous, Maria. If my father finds out I know him..." I trail off, trying to sound calm.

"Not him, the brother. I think my ovaries are on fire."

Maria's eyes are glued to the back of the brother, and I can't help but laugh.

"You're impossible."

She nudges me, tilting her head toward the men. "Maybe, but tall, dark, and deadly is looking straight at you, and he's removed his mask."

Quickly, my gaze finds him, heart skipping. Sure enough, Raphael is staring right at me. He smiles, just a flash, enough to send a thrill through me, and then says something to his brother before they slip inside.

"*This. Is. Bad,*" I say, dragging out each word for dramatic effect.

"Oh, calm down. The only people who know about you two are me, you, and him."

"Your brother, V, was there."

Maria waves a hand dismissively. "Vincent won't say a word. Besides, he was outside. He's around here somewhere. We could go find him?"

I nod, exhaling. "Let's. I don't want him saying the wrong thing to a member of my family. I'll be locked up forever."

Her hands land on my shoulders, steadying me. "Calm down. If your father locks you up, I promise to break you out." She crosses her heart, then holds out her pinky finger.

I hook mine with hers. We've been doing this since we were kids—always looking out for each other.

"Let's find V," I say, feeling just a little braver with her at my side.

CHAPTER
Three

Raphael

The air in Hector Chavez's office is heavy with cigar smoke and polished oak. It sticks to the back of my throat and curls around my senses, a warning I've known all my life—this is power, distilled, and I am small in its presence.

My father, massive and immovable, sits next to Hector on a leather sofa, fingers steepled, eyes calculating. Hector leans back in his seat, one hand holding a glass of amber liquid, the other resting on the back of the sofa. Both men are smiling, but not casually. Proud. Dangerous. Like hunters watching a wounded animal stumble straight into their trap.

"Raphael," my father says, voice low and smooth, almost buttery. "Sit."

I lower myself onto the chair, stiff, arms at my sides. My muscles are taut, ready to bolt. Ready to punch. Ready to do anything to protect myself, my father, and my family.

"We've come to a decision," my father says, eyes narrowing slightly, measuring me.

"Yes," Hector adds, voice calm, practiced. "You and Sophia can end decades of rivalry between our families. Permanently. Strategically."

My pulse spikes. My stomach twists. I know exactly where this is going, and every fiber of my being resists.

"You've arranged a marriage," I say before I can stop myself. The words taste like bile in my mouth. "You can't, there has to be another way."

Hector's laughter is smooth, almost musical, as it slides over me like ice. "Raphael, we're not punishing you. We're securing a legacy. Our families united will be stronger than ever. You and Sophia together, you'll be unstoppable."

Leaning forward, my voice is sharp. "Stronger

for who? For you? For him?" I gesture to both older men. "My life isn't some prize to be handed over."

My father inclines his head slightly, a slow, deliberate movement. "Raphael, you've always had a way with women. Sophia... she's exceptional. She'll be your partner. Don't mistake my words for cruelty. This is a strategy. A legacy. An opportunity."

I laugh, bitterly. "Opportunity? You mean control. You mean using a person to secure your power." My chest tightens. "She's not a chess piece. She's not a prize. She's a person. And I won't—"

"She is all of that," Hector interrupts, his voice sounds like silk over steel. "And more. Intelligent. Capable. Beautiful. She is perfect for this... *arrangement*. And you, Raphael, are perfect for her. You will protect her, or this union will dissolve into war."

I clench my jaw. Her name echoes in my mind. The way she moves. The way she's oblivious to the magnetism she holds over me and those around her.

"I can't be... *forced into this*," I spit, leaning

back. "I won't. There has to be another solution. There has to be a—"

Hector shakes his head, slow and deliberate. "There isn't. Not for the future. Not for peace. Not for strength."

Hector's hand moves to the crystal decanter beside him. He lifts it, tilts it toward me without pouring, just a gesture. "Raphael... we're stepping aside. The future will be yours to lead. But make no mistake... my sons, they will hold high positions in the combined family. Their power will be unquestionable to everyone but you. Their loyalty secured. Together, the Costa and Chavez families will dominate. No one will challenge us. Our rule will be absolute."

My chest tightens, the weight of their words pressing down on me like iron. I've been trained to take responsibility, to carry the family legacy. To command. But this... this is different. This isn't about skill or honor. This is destiny forced upon me.

"And Sophia?" I ask, voice quietly. "What about her? Does she even know? Has she—"

"She will be informed," Hector says casually, like it's a detail easily handled. "But you..." His eyes gleam, sharp. "You *will* make this work. She has been sheltered all of her life. Not allowed to date. Sophia is untouched and a good age for children."

I blink. My fists clench. I stand, pacing the length of the office, feeling the marble under my boots, the weight of expectation pressing on me. "I don't even know if I can. If I *should*..."

Both men watch, satisfied, proud. Like I'm a chess piece, moving exactly as planned.

"You have time to consider," my father says, voice low, menacingly calm. "But not long. Tonight, both families are gathered here. Everything is arranged. You *will* marry before the night ends."

"How? There are licenses to get, a priest, a million other things. Hell, a wedding dress."

Hector waves a hand. "As your father said, everything is arranged."

I stop. The words echo like a gunshot in the silent room. *Tonight?* My mind scrambles. My chest tightens. My thoughts collide... *Sophia. My responsibility. My desire. My anger. My fear.*

I run a hand over my face, trying to find rationality, trying to find a way to breathe, to think, to fight. But my thoughts keep returning to her.

I can't.

I shouldn't.

But I do want her.

And if last year was anything to go by, Sophia is not as sheltered as her father thinks.

Taking a deep breath, I walk toward the door, needing to escape the weight, needing to find air that isn't tainted with cigar smoke and power. Each step feels heavy. My mind races with thoughts. *How do I even face her? How do I... explain?*

The hallway outside the office is quieter than I expected. The party outside hums faintly, muffled, irrelevant. I pace, muttering to myself under my breath, hands twitching, fists clenching, every instinct screaming.

Then I see her.

Sophia. Masked, radiant, unaware. She stands near the grand doorway, costume perfect, posture effortless. I stop dead, heart hammering. My mind freezes.

Her gaze lifts, meeting mine.

For a moment, I can't breathe. I can't move. I

can't think.

She smiles small, subtle, unknowing, and it feels like the world tilts.

With the next step I take toward her, my chest tightens, my mind screams, every rational thought colliding with instinct. Every fiber of my being wants to protect her, to claim her, but also to warn her.

I am supposed to marry her.

And yet, every second of hesitation makes me wonder if I'm already too late.

I stop in front of her. She tilts her head slightly with curiosity behind her mask. The air between us feels electric.

I want to speak.

I want to move.

I want to escape.

But I don't.

Because just for a moment, standing there, looking at her, I realize how impossible this is going to be.

CHAPTER
Four

Sophia

The soft echo of shoes on polished floors alerts me before I see him.

Raphael.

Every instinct in my body tightens. He moves with the cold precision I've only heard whispered about—*The Reaper.* And now, he's walking straight toward me.

His shoulders are rigid, jaw sharp under the dim light, his dark hair falling just enough to shadow the edge of his eyes but not enough to hide that warning expression. *Don't cross me.* Raphael's lips are pressed into a straight line, and yet my pulse stutters.

He stops a foot away. I feel his heat even across the small space. Before I can move, he reaches out, taking my hand with a grip that's firm and unyielding.

My heart lurches. "Raphael—" I start, but he pulls me along as though I've been waiting for this without knowing it. My fingers press into his hand, and his hold is like iron.

We move through the house where the walls are lined with art and trophies, and there is a faint scent of leather in the air. My mind screams, but my body follows. He doesn't ask and doesn't wait for me.

At the end of the corridor, he opens a door and steps aside. The room is dim, a single chandelier casting long shadows over polished wood floors. Heavy curtains block the night, and a faint gleam of party lights sneaks through. A leather armchair sits angled toward a grand desk, papers stacked neatly. The lingering scent of sandalwood and iron hangs in the air—my brother Antonio's office.

Raphael steps in behind me, closing the door softly but firmly, then locks it. His eyes scan the room before landing on me. Even in the quiet, he radiates control.

"You need to understand," he says, low, deliberate. "Both families have decided. There's no room for negotiation."

I nod, my heart thundering in my ears. Every nerve screams to run, but my legs won't obey.

"You think your father would protect you from this?" he continues. "He won't. You've lived under his watch. Your life has been arranged to serve his plans."

Confused, I shake my head. He notices, steps forward to take my hand in his. Raphael's touch is gentle, impossibly so. My eyes lift to his, searching for the cold killer I've heard about. Instead, I find something more complicated. Far more dangerous.

Without warning, his lips are on mine. I freeze, wanting to pull back, yet the heat, the magnetic pull, the dangerous weight of him, ignites something I cannot name. My chest presses into his, body responding despite my protests.

Raphael breaks the kiss, eyes dark, unreadable. "Tonight, you will be *mine*. And as my wife, I will protect you. But you *will* do as you are told."

The room shrinks. His presence presses in from all sides. I want to tell him he's wrong, but my voice has abandoned me. The only thing I can think of doing is moving away from him.

"Wife?"

"You think you have a choice?" he asks, closing the gap. "Your father, my father... they've conspired. And I—" His heat makes it real.

I press my hands to my chest, trying to steady my heart. "My father—"

"They planned this," he interrupts, tilting my face gently with a hand. "Both families, united. You are my bride tonight, and together we will stop years of bloodshed."

The weight of it crashes into me. My life, orchestrated like a symphony, and I, the finale. Fear and desire clash, a dizzying cocktail I cannot escape.

"You're perfect," he murmurs, his thumb brushing my cheek. "Exactly what they wanted. Exactly what *I* want."

I want to pull away. But I cannot. The gravity of him, the danger, the controlled presence, roots me to the spot.

His lips meet mine again, slower and more deliberate. Raphael ignites a spark I cannot deny. Barriers crumble under his attention. His hands on my waist, holding, firm but not crushing, chest rising and falling against mine. My confusion melts into something fiery, dizzying, and undeniable.

When he breaks the kiss, breath warm against mine, he whispers, "Tonight, every part of you is *mine*. In return, you will be safe... but you *will* obey. That is the balance."

My chest rises and falls in quick succession. I want to argue, to scream, to flee, but the magnetic pull, the undeniable connection, holds me captive.

"I... I don't know if I can," I admit.

"I know," he murmurs. "But tonight, there is no choice. You are my bride. And I will claim you, in every way, as is my right."

Stumbling back, I'm desperate for control, for air, for reason. He watches, calm, unshaken, every inch the man whispered about—the killer, the enforcer, dangerous and precise. Nothing like the man I met a year ago, who kissed me until I was dizzy and made me feel special.

Raphael brushes a thumb along my cheek, tracing my jaw. My knees threaten to buckle, but he holds me steady, syncing with my pulse.

"Raphael…" I breathe, trembling.

"Yes?" His eyes darken, intensity unmatched.

"When? When does this… marriage… start?"

He tilts his head, ghost of a smile teasing his lips. "In an hour. Everything is arranged."

His words crash over me.

My mind freezes.

My heart hammers violently.

I want to scream, to run, to fight.

But I can't.

Not yet.

Nothing will *ever* be the same again.

CHAPTER Five

Raphael

Walking beside Sophia, her hand brushes against mine for the briefest moment, and I feel the heat flicker under my skin. The night air is thick with tension, and I hear the faint hum of voices from outside the mansion. I knock on the door to her father's study, open it, and usher her inside. Sophia glances at me as I close the door.

Her voice is loud as she says, "Father! You cannot. This is insane! I won't—"

I freeze, listening to her protests, the anger, the fear, and something else—*determination.* She's sharp, unbroken, and I admire that in her.

Tonight *is* going to happen whether she wants it to or not. I begin to think about how I can make this easier for her.

Closing my eyes for a heartbeat, I then let them drift across the party outside, and they land on Maria, in her Ursula costume. She's laughing at something Gabriel says. And Gabriel, my brother, leaning in, is completely smitten. They're both flirting so openly it's almost vulgar, and yet I can't help the corner of my mouth lifting.

I stalk across the lawn, my presence drawing their attention. Maria turns first. Her smile falters when she sees me, curiosity flickering in her eyes.

"Maria," I say, voice low, commanding. "Come with me."

Her brows rise, but she doesn't hesitate. I glance at Gabriel. "You too," I add.

His jaw tightens, but he follows.

We find a quiet spot tucked between the trimmed hedges and fountains, where the night feels a little more private.

"Something's happening," I say, my voice low but steady. "Tonight, Sophia's life changes, whether she wants it to or not. Both families have come to an agreement. We... we are to be married." I shake my head, letting the weight of it sink in. "We are going to be husband and wife."

Maria blinks at me, confusion written all over her face. "Wait... what do you mean? What's happening?"

Gabriel stiffens, shock written across every line of him. "Yeah, Raphael, explain. She's going to be what?"

"My wife."

Maria and Gabriel exchange a glance.

He frowns. "You can't be serious?"

"Deadly serious." I fix him with a look that brooks no argument. "Gabriel, I want you as my best man. I trust no one else to stand with me for her."

He swallows hard but nods, jaw tight. Loyalty runs deep in him, but so does his shock.

Then my eyes return to Maria. She's still staring at me with disbelief and something else that makes my chest tighten.

"She's going to need you tonight," I say. "Go up to her room. Clean off that Ursula makeup. Stand next to her. Be her anchor. She can get through this evening with you by her side."

"How?" Maria asks, and I know she's talking

about the wedding.

I run a hand through my hair, sighing.

Before I can answer, Gabriel lets out a humorless laugh. "It's why we're here, isn't it? The two families coming together as one." He rests a hand on my shoulder. "You can say no."

"But I can't. It will end the war and unite both families. It's for the best."

Maria's gaze softens. *I'm hoping she understands.* "I'll go find Sophia."

"I left her in her father's study. She can't run, Maria. There will be consequences. Try to get her through this."

"She's my best friend. I'll do what's best for her. *Always.*"

She leaves us at a run. I watch her go, hoping she'll do the right thing.

By being at Sophia's side, she doesn't have to face this alone.

CHAPTER Six

Sophia

My bedroom feels like a prison. The walls, once comforting with their prints of the Louvre, Parisian cobblestone streets, and the Eiffel Tower, now mock me. Each image of freedom, of a life I had imagined, feels like a cruel joke. When this wedding happens, I'll be at Raphael's beck and call. I'll never get to go anywhere, do anything for myself. My father spelled it out in simple English, even if he didn't say the words, that I'm nothing but a brood mare.

Tears streak down my cheeks as I stare at what I once believed would be my sanctuary, my home.

The future I dreamed of is slipping through my fingers like sand. My gaze falls on the white wedding dress hanging on my walk-in closet door. Every woman dreams of this moment, *her wedding day*, to the man she loves, the walk down the aisle. *Mine?* Halloween costumes and a man who kills for his empire. A man who will display me like a trophy, just as my father does.

A sudden crash of the door slamming against the wall makes me jump. Maria bursts in, eyes wide and frantic, and grabs my hands. "Pack a bag. We don't have much time."

"What?" My voice trembles.

"Move it, Sophia!" She doesn't wait for me to argue. She strides to my dressing table, lifts my mother's jewelry box with care, and sets it on the bed. "You'll want this, right?"

I blink at her, speechless. "What? What are you doing?"

"Busting you out, of course!" Her voice is fierce, but there's a tremor in it that betrays her fear. "It's one thing to flirt with The Reaper, it's another thing entirely to marry him."

Her eyes glisten with tears as she moves into my closet and emerges with a small, black suitcase. "What do you want to take?"

"They'll come after me. It's useless."

"Yep," she says, her jaw set tight. "They will. But we'll be long gone before they even know we're missing."

"Maria, you're not listening. There is *no* escape."

Her hands ball into fists and land firmly on her hips. Even with the 'Ursula' makeup smeared across her face, she looks like a warrior ready for battle.

"We. Are. Leaving."

"Maria—" I try again, my voice barely above a whisper, but she cuts me off.

"No!" She storms back into the closet and tosses a T-shirt at me. "Put that on," she commands, then flips open a chest of drawers with a sharp pull. "And these jeans."

I catch the garments, heartbeat kicking wildly in my chest. "This is insane," I whisper, my words barely audible.

"Insane?" she spits back, eyes blazing. "You think it's sane to marry a man who would kill without hesitation? To let your life be dictated by your father like a chess piece?"

I can't find the words. I just stare at her, at the fire burning in her gaze. My chest tightens, and a shaky breath escapes me.

Maria crouches to meet my eyes, voice softer now, almost a plea. "Sophia... you have a choice. Take it. Run with me. Please."

I swallow hard, trembling. Somewhere deep in my chest, a tiny spark of hope flickers.

"Okay."

Maria smiles. "Good. Now, stand up so I can undo your dress. We don't have much time."

Maria and I move quickly through the dimly lit halls, our footsteps muffled against the carpet. My heart beats so loud I'm sure anyone nearby could hear it. The suitcase swings against my leg, but Maria's grip on my hand is firm, guiding me toward the back door.

We slip outside, and relief floods me for a brief second—freedom feels close enough to touch. My eyes sweep the backyard, taking in the familiar shadows, the hedges, the moonlight glinting off the grass. We walk at a normal pace until we are out of the lights of the house, then we break into a run toward the fence at the back of the grounds. Maria goes through first while I keep my eyes peeled for my family's security or anyone else who might recognize me.

And then my stomach drops.

The back gates are wide open.

Four guards lie sprawled on the ground, motionless. Blood stains the grass beneath them. My breath catches, and I stumble back, horror tightening my chest.

I exchange a look with Maria. She swallows hard, her face pale, but her jaw is set. She grabs my hand and starts to pull me along.

"Come on, Sophia! We don't have time. If we stay, you'll be trapped."

I stop, yanking my hand free. "I can't let my family get hurt. I can't just leave them." My voice shakes with a mixture of fear and anger. "I'm angry at my family, yes, but I can't... I can't let them be harmed... or worse!"

Maria's eyes widen, panic flickering there. "Sophia, we *have* to go! We don't know how many more—"

"I don't care!" My chest is heaving. "I can't turn my back on this."

Before Maria can protest, I bolt back toward the house, my suitcase forgotten on the lawn. Every step feels like my heart is going to burst from my chest. I skid around the corner and—

He's there.

Raphael.

My body collides with his, and his arms catch me instinctively. I feel the heat radiating off him.

"Raphael... there's trouble," I gasp.

"Trouble?" His brow furrows. "What?"

"I-I was leaving..." The words tumble out, desperate and chaotic. "The back gates... the guards... they're all dead."

His eyes narrow as he scans the backyard, then back at me. He notices the slight movement behind me and turns sharply. Maria, no longer in her costume, stands frozen, hesitation written across her face.

For a heartbeat, his expression is pure, white-hot anger. "Maria, were you helping her to escape?"

I grab his hand, tugging at him. "No... look." My voice is urgent, panicked. "It's not about me. *Both families are in danger."*

The anger in his eyes doesn't vanish, but the icy calculation returns. His jaw tightens, and he swears under his breath, a low, deadly sound.

"Both families..." he mutters, his hand tightening around mine. "Show me."

I nod, my chest heaving, my heartbeat hammering in my ears. The backyard stretches before us, shadows pooling around the hedges and trees. Maria lingers a step behind, hesitating, but I know she loves me enough to stay, enough to trust me as we move toward the men.

Raphael crouches beside the nearest one, his movements deliberate, precise. He leans closer, fingers brushing against the man's neck, then pauses to open his jacket. Empty. The gun holster is bare. My stomach twists.

Raphael reaches into his jacket and swears. *"Fuck."*

"What?" I ask.

"I left my fucking phone in the car."

"Do you have a gun?" I whisper, careful not to sound too loud.

"No. We were told to come unarmed."

Swallowing hard, I look back at the house. "I

know where my family keeps theirs."

His gaze locks on me. "Can you shoot?"

I nod, forcing steadiness into my voice. "Yes. Dad always said I should know how to take care of myself." I glance over my shoulder at Maria, who shifts uneasily. "Maria does too. She's a better shot than I am."

Maria shakes her head, a faint, nervous laugh escaping her. "Not on my best day."

I shrug, a tight laugh of my own. "We've only ever shot at targets. But we can help."

"Good," he says, eyes scanning every shadow, every inch of the yard like it might erupt into violence. "Lead the way."

CHAPTER Seven

Raphael

It irks me that the women are leading the way. I don't know this house, don't know where the Chavez family keeps their weapons. If they're anything like my family, it will be well hidden— probably in the basement. Law enforcement would have a field day if they ever found it. No one wants to go down for gun possession, even if it's an arsenal that could start a small war.

Sophia opens a door under the staircase, revealing an elevator. She hits the button, and the door slides open immediately.

We step inside, and I glance down at her,

noting the way her fingers twitch ever so slightly with anticipation, fear, maybe both. "Is there another way in and out?" I ask, my voice low.

"Yes, but this is quicker," she says, calm but tense.

Nodding, I press further. "Where is the exit when the doors open? Left, right, or straight?"

"Why do you ask?"

"If I were behind this, I'd know where your guns are, and I'd already have someone waiting for us," I reply, watching the flicker of fear pass across her eyes.

"Fuck," Maria whispers, clutching Sophia's hand like it's a lifeline.

"The stairs are to the left," Sophia says, her voice barely above a breath.

I don't wait for instructions, pressing Sophia against the side wall of the elevator, my stance firm, protective. Maria steps next to her. With shoulders squared, eyes scanning the gap between the elevator doors, I plant myself opposite them. If anyone is waiting, they might assume the space is empty, which may be enough of a delay to give us a chance.

The doors slide open. Sophia's gaze meets

mine, wide and unguarded. We're exposed. I hold my breath, waiting for the first sign of movement from the darkened room beyond.

Nothing.

Silence.

The doors begin to close.

At the last possible moment, I slam my hand out, stopping them.

Stepping forward, I hold a hand up, signaling the women to wait. Every muscle in my body tightens. My shoes scrape softly against the polished wood floor. I move inch by inch, ears straining, picking up the slightest shift in the air. Shadows cling to corners, but nothing stirs. The door to the room beyond remains shut.

"We're good," I finally whisper, relief threading through me. My eyes sweep over them, making sure they feel it too.

"Does this mean we're safe?" Maria asks, her voice is low and unsure.

"No. It means they aren't as cautious as me," I reply, my gaze scanning the space again.

The room is set up like a theater with raised chairs facing a large television mounted on the wall, bookcases on either side filled with novels and trinkets. To the left, a bar stocked with spirits gleams under the soft lighting. To the right, a popcorn machine stands ready, surrounded by packets of candy and stacked bars of chocolate.

Sophia glides past me to the television and presses a button. One of the bookcases shudders and slides forward, revealing a hidden room beyond.

"Are you coming?" she asks.

I follow her inside, my eyes adjusting to the dim light. The small room smells faintly of oil and metal. It's tight, crowded, but meticulously organized.

Rows of weapons line the walls with guns of every size and type, each with a purpose. My fingers twitch, itching to touch them, to feel their weight.

There are Glocks in various calibers, sleek and deadly, ready to spit rounds with frightening precision. Next to them, compact pistols, which can be easily hidden, quick to draw, but lethal at close range. Machine guns hang from brackets above, their barrels long and cold, capable of tearing through a room in seconds. Shotguns sit low, in the shelves, perfect for clearing halls or enforcing territory.

Boxes of ammunition are stacked neatly, each labeled: 9mm, .45, 5.56, .308. Knives in sheaths glint under the low light, from standard combat knives to serrated survival blades. And then there are the more unusual pieces. There is a crossbow tucked into a corner, silencers lined up on a shelf, and a handful of small revolvers with a finish so polished they almost seem ceremonial.

I run my gaze over everything again, noting which ones would be fastest in my hands. The Glock in .45, light enough for quick flicks, heavy enough to keep recoil manageable. An Uzi leaning in the corner—small, compact, lethal if the situation turns chaotic. The AR-15 is loaded and ready, its stock adjusted perfectly for whoever trained here. Every piece tells a story— calculated, prepared, and incredibly lethal.

Sophia tilts her head, watching me. "You like what you see?"

I smirk, keeping my voice low. "I like that someone's planning for more than just dinner and drinks." My eyes flick back to the shadows at the doorway. "But I still don't trust the silence. Whoever killed the men at the gate must have a plan."

The air feels thick, almost electric, as the women each pick a gun. My fingers brush against cold metal as I lift a Glock and a pump-action shotgun from the racks. I slide bullets and shells into my coat pockets.

"You should each take a smaller pistol," I say, keeping my voice low. "And hide it on your person, along with bullets for reloading. You don't want to be caught without ammo if shit hits the fan."

Maria nods, eyes sharp, and grabs a compact 9mm. She tucks it into the back pocket of her jeans. Sophia drapes a strap over her shoulder and hooks it onto a shotgun, the barrel resting heavy against her side. She grabs a box of shells, shoving some into her pockets, before picking up a small Walter PPK and sliding it into the back of her jeans.

"You sure you can handle that?" I ask, nodding toward the shotgun balanced against her chest.

Her smirk is confident, even under the low light. "Recoil is a bitch," she says, testing the weight with a tilt of her shoulder. "But yes, I'll be fine."

I glance at them, noting the way they move, the way Maria's fingers brush the trigger lightly, almost ritualistically, and the way Sophia's shoulders tense and relax, readying herself. The small details matter. Every twitch, every micro-movement could be the difference between getting out clean or not.

I check the ammo one more time, feeling the reassuring click of cartridges sliding into the magazine. The Glock's grip fits perfectly in my hand, and the shotgun's pump is familiar under my fingers. I glance at the women again. They're ready, or as ready as anyone can be.

"You know..." I say, smirking despite the tension, "... if anyone tries something, they're going to regret it."

Maria raises an eyebrow, a ghost of a grin on her lips. "We've got this, right?"

"Right," I say, though worry gnaws at me for both women.

"Which way do we go? The elevator or the stairs?" Sophia asks, her voice tight.

"The elevator," I answer without hesitation.

Maria walks ahead, but I grab Sophia's hand, holding her back. "If things go sideways, you stay behind me. Got it?"

"Ensuring your bride isn't hurt?" she asks, bitterness coating her words.

"Ensuring the woman I've obsessed over for a year doesn't get hurt before I have the privilege of becoming her husband." My voice is low, steady, but there's no mistaking the intensity behind it.

Her mouth drops open, and I take a step back toward the elevator. When she joins us, her face is red, a mixture of embarrassment and fury I can't help but find... *captivating.*

Maria hits the button for the elevator, and the doors slide open with a soft hiss. We step inside together, the metal walls reflecting the faint light. I pray silently that nothing has started upstairs that we are not aware of, and that we are walking straight into chaos.

"I need you to call your brother, Antonio," I say.

"If we go to his office, I can use the phone in there," Sophia replies, her eyes darting toward me.

"Where is your phone?" I ask, keeping my tone even.

"We ditched them to escape," Maria states flatly.

"Remind me to thank you for that later," I say, staring at her with a cold intensity. No humor in my gaze.

"Hey," Sophia snaps, stepping closer to Maria. "Don't you go picking on her. She's *my* friend, and she was protecting *me*."

I glance at Sophia, noting the flush in her cheeks and the sharp edge in her voice. I can almost hear the unspoken challenge beneath it, and it makes my chest tighten. Protecting her—no, both of them—isn't just duty, it's an overwhelming compulsion. If Sophia cares for Maria, then I do too.

The doors to the elevator slide open, and no one is waiting. I press a finger to my lips, signaling the women to stay quiet, then slip out and push open the hidden door under the stairs. I peer into the hallway—*empty*—and nothing stirs. I step lightly, ears straining, scanning every shadow.

Glancing back, I signal for them to follow. Sophia steps forward, moving ahead of me, and I shake my head. "No."

"I know how to get through my house without being seen. You don't," she whispers.

I close my eyes, nodding. Doesn't mean I have to like it. I don't. But she's right, Sophia knows this house better than I ever could.

When Maria moves to pass me, I grab her arm, shake my head, and slot her behind me.

"Fine," Maria whispers loudly, just enough for me to hear.

I glance over my shoulder, eyes sharp. "And don't shoot me if things get real."

Maria stifles a laugh, a quick, nervous sound. "*Well*... that'd be one way to stop the wedding."

I let a corner of a smirk slip, though the tension in my chest doesn't ease.

And while we are moving through the house, guided by Sophia's familiarity, I can only pray my instincts and my guns are enough to keep them safe.

There are so many hidden passages in this house that I'm glad I let Sophia lead. Every step she takes, every turn she knows, makes my chest tighten in both relief and frustration.

Relief that she knows where she's going.

Frustration that I don't.

When we marry and have a home of our own, there will be at least one hidden passage. Just in case anything happens, so we can escape.

Finally, we step into Antonio's office, and I lock the door behind us. Sophia is pacing, phone pressed to her ear.

"Antonio, I need you to come to your office."

A pause. She rolls her eyes, muttering under her breath.

"No, it has nothing to do with the wedding. But I'm pissed at you for not telling me."

Another pause, longer this time. Her fingers tighten around the phone.

"Can you just get your ass in here, *please*?"

She slams the phone down and glares at me, eyes blazing. "He's coming."

I nod once and remain silent. My gaze sweeps over the office, noting the angles, the doors, the possible exits. As much as I want to tell Sophia to relax, to trust me, I know better. Marrying me wasn't something she wanted. My mind drifts back to last Halloween when she was in my arms, and right now it feels like a lifetime ago. My job right now is to keep them both alive until we get through this.

I sweep the office again, one door leads to the hallway, and one window to the outside. If I smash the window or shoot it out, we could escape through it. My fingers brush the Glock in my hand, and I check the shotgun slung over my shoulder.

Sophia paces near the desk, her stance tense, phone forgotten for the moment. Maria hovers behind me, fingers twitching as if she wants to check her pistol.

If this hits the fan, I'll take the center, using the desk as partial cover. Shotguns pack a punch at close range, and the Glock is quick if we have to move.

I can almost hear my heartbeat in the quiet, loud against the hum of the air conditioning. My eyes flick to Sophia, and the frown that mars her pretty face.

Someone tries to open the door, then a sharp knock rattles it.

"Sis, you in there?"

Sophia moves toward it, but I hold up a hand, gesturing for both women to step behind me. They do, quick and tense, and I push the door open just enough. Antonio strides through, shoulders squared, eyes sharp. I slam the door behind him and lock it. His gaze locks on the Glock in my hand, and before I can say a word, he swings, and his fist impacts with my jaw.

"No!" Sophia shouts, stepping between us, only to land flat on her ass. "Oh, for fuck's sake, Antonio. *Stop it!*"

We break apart, and Maria is between us. "Ant, you have to stop. Raphael is not the enemy."

"Antonio," he hisses at her, tension curling in every syllable.

"If you stop, I promise to never call you Ant again."

Antonio glares, jaw tight. "What the fuck is going on?"

I hold up a hand, laying the Glock on his desk, but my grip on the shotgun never loosens. "Your sister and her best friend were trying to escape—"

"So, you thought you'd take matters into your own hands and stop them?" His voice thunders, booming in the office.

I suck in a deep breath, letting the weight of the situation settle before I speak. "No. If you'll notice, both women have guns."

Antonio's eyes snap to Sophia, then Maria, who's waving her pistol in the air with a mischievous grin.

"Will someone tell me *what the fuck* is going on?" Antonio asks, hands on his hips, gaze piercing through me.

"Well, if you'd let Raphael finish instead of interrupting, we would," Sophia fires back, voice sharp.

Antonio circles the desk, sits down, leans back, and crosses his arms. "Fine. Speak."

I rub my jaw, tension tightening in my shoulders. "At the back of your property... they found your security team. All of them. Dead."

Silence falls in the room. Antonio blinks, then leans forward, voice low but deadly. "Dead? Who the fuck—"

Tightening my grip on the shotgun, letting him see the steel in my eyes, I interrupt him, "I don't know. That's why we're here. To make sure it doesn't happen to us."

"Who else knew that both families would be here tonight?" Sophia asks.

Antonio leans forward, elbows on his desk. "Everyone who got an invite." He stands. "This is not talk for women."

Sophia laughs. "I forgot. We just use women as broodmares and marry them off. Don't be such a dick, Antonio. You need us."

Maria moves to stand next to Sophia.

"A man does not stand behind a woman for protection," replies Antonio.

"No, but a woman could stand next to him," I say.

Sophia gives me the briefest of smiles, but it falls all too quickly from her face.

"We don't know who it is or how many are outside. We can only assume someone is moving against us."

Antonio frowns at me and points. "How do we know your family isn't behind this?"

"How do I know yours isn't, and you killed your own men to make it look like it was us?"

Antonio holds my gaze and finally nods. "The deal between your father and mine has been in the works for six months. I don't think either of them would risk it over some power play."

"No, but *you* might." My words slice through the air.

He chuckles, low and easy, then glances at his

sister. "Sophia, tell Raphael how much I love working for our father."

"You hate it," she says, her voice firm. "You don't want to run the family."

I can't help it, I laugh. "You expect me to believe that you actually shared this with your sister? You're like me. Groomed to take over from the day you were born." I pick up the Glock and then lean against his desk.

Antonio smirks, then moves deliberately around his desk, opens a drawer, and pulls out two Glocks, laying them on the surface. "Exactly. It's why the deal happened. Neither I nor my brothers want the crown. Papa faced a choice... hand the family over to some loyal soldier who isn't blood, or merge with the Costas and put you in charge."

I frown, shaking my head. "It doesn't make sense."

He grunts, checking the weapons. The sounds are sharp in the quiet room. "It's how Papa saves face. Territories stay the same, your people stay in place, ours stay in place. Only now, instead of butting heads, we work together."

I cock my head, studying him. "Why don't you

want it?"

"Angelica," Sophia murmurs, almost reverently, and Antonio's expression tightens.

"Yeah," he says, voice rougher now. "She wants no part of the family business. She agreed to marry me, but she won't let me put a target on her back or on our kids. No children growing up in this house. Not like us."

I tilt my head, incredulous. "You're giving it all up... for a woman?"

Antonio smiles, slow and knowing, like he's been waiting for this. "She's not just any woman."

I let that hang, studying him.

The room feels smaller somehow, the tension thick, and Sophia says, "For some people, love's important."

"Yeah," he says, eyes flicking to Sophia and then back to me. "For some, it's the only thing that matters."

"Who then?" I ask.

Antonio tilts his head back, eyes on the ceiling. His fingers tighten around the triggers of the Glocks in each hand. Slowly, he lowers them, his gaze locking onto mine. "Have you had any run-ins with the Russians?"

I nod, my jaw tight. "Yeah. They've been moving in, pushing their tainted shit to some of our dealers."

"Tainted?" Sophia asks.

"Carfentanil," I say flatly, letting the weight of the word hang in the air. "They're giving it away to a few of our dealers. Free. The catch? It'll kill you. Hell, even a little on your skin could do it. They're trying to push us out. Dealers and clients are dropping like flies. Makes the cops hungry for a bust, thinking it's us."

Sophia's eyes widen, and she glances at Antonio. "Is that... *our* problem too?"

He nods, the movement slow, deliberate. "They don't care whose turf it is. Death sells fear. Fear sells power. And they're trying to scare everyone into submission. We either stop them, or we get buried under it."

I lean forward, pressing my palms to the desk. "And you think they'll hit us directly?"

Antonio shrugs, a faint smirk tugging at the corner of his mouth. "Maybe. But they're smart, they know the cops are looking at us. Our deaths would just make them targets. The shrewd move is chaos first, then control."

"You mean they start shooting, we all start shooting at each other, and the only ones left are the Russians, so they can take over?" I spit the words out, tasting the bitterness.

Sophia shifts, tugging nervously at her sleeve. "So... what do we do?"

I glance at her, then back at Antonio. "We hit them before they hit us. *Hard*. Make sure everyone knows the Costas and the Chavez families aren't soft."

Antonio tucks one Glock into the back of his trousers. "I like the sound of that. But you're going to need more than firepower, Raphael. These Russians... they play dirty."

I let a slow grin creep across my face, the kind that always makes men in the room shift uneasily. "Good. So do I."

There's a beat of silence, thick and heavy. Leaning back, I let the Glock rest on my thigh and study them both. "How do we warn our families?"

Antonio's eyes glint. "Sophia, could you go out and ask Papa and Mr. Costa to come inside?"

"I don't want her getting hurt." The words slip out before I can stop them.

"We need to let them know. Dressed like

that…" he looks her up and down, "… both men will come inside."

"I don't like it," I say.

Antonio shakes his head. "Sophia, what do you say?"

She takes a slow breath and shoulders the weight of it. "Antonio is right." She sets the shotgun down. "You aren't head of this family yet. I don't take orders from you. But if something were to happen to either man, war would ensue."

Maria clears her throat. "I'll go with her. We can just take the pistols. No one will even realize we have them."

"Perfect," I say, my sarcasm sharp enough to cut glass, and I glance at Antonio. "Need I remind you that this deal between our families only works if I marry Sophia? If she gets herself killed, we're back to the way we were."

Sophia swallows hard, the tremor in her jaw betraying her fear, but she nods. "I… I can do it."

"Good," I say, my tone flat, like a blade. "Because the next time someone dies, I want it to be them, not us."

Antonio leans back, a sly grin creeping over his face. "And I thought today would be boring."

"No such thing as boring when the Russians are in town. Let's make sure they remember why we run this city." My fingers tighten around the Glock, the steel cold against my palm, and the thought of losing her—*my obsession*—sends a chill straight through me.

Sophia and Maria move toward the door, careful but determined. I watch every step, every twitch of muscle, every flinch. My eyes flick to Antonio, who's watching them leave.

"Act natural." My voice stops Sophia, and she looks at me. "You're a spitfire. Make a scene. Demand that both men come inside, and if it looks like they won't, raise your voice. They won't want to be embarrassed in front of their men and the other guests."

Sophia gives me the briefest of smiles. "I can do that."

I point at Maria. "And if you can, get my brother, Gabriel, to come inside with you. Say, 'chalice.' If he doesn't come, tell him, 'Raphael has sipped from the poison chalice.' "

"Code word?" asks Antonio.

"Yes, something we've done since he was young. A way to let me know if he's in trouble."

"Got it," replies Maria.

Reaching out, I put a hand on each of their shoulders. "Be careful, both of you."

CHAPTER
Eight

Sophia

"Weirdest Halloween ever," Maria says as we weave through the crowd at the front of my home.

"Yep," I reply. "And I thought marrying Raphael was the strangest thing that was going to happen tonight."

Maria nudges me. "Gabriel's over there, talking to Vincent."

I glance across the yard and spot them. "Let's divide and conquer."

"Okay, but don't get yourself killed," she warns, giving my shoulder a quick squeeze.

We hug, tight enough to feel the tension in her chest, then I make a beeline for my father. He's got a woman draped on one arm and is chatting with an older family friend.

"Mario, it's so good to see you." I kiss both his cheeks, and he sizes me up with that calculating look that always makes my skin prickle.

"Sophia, where's your costume?" he asks, his voice sharp but teasing.

He's dressed like Gomez Addams with slicked-back hair and a pinstripe suit, and his wife, no doubt, will be dressed as Morticia. The woman with my father looks like she's trying to be Marilyn Monroe, but the wig is all wrong, slipping slightly over her eyes.

"Yes, Sophia," Papa says, narrowing his gaze at me. "Why aren't you dressed?"

I take a breath, smile sweetly, and keep my tone light. "Papa, there's been a slight change of plans. Raphael and Antonio want to speak with you inside."

He arches an eyebrow. "Is that so?"

"Yes, Papa. We should hurry before they kill each other," I say, giving Mario and the younger woman a polite smile that doesn't quite reach my eyes.

Papa pats the woman's hand and nods toward Mario. "Family business. I'll be back shortly."

Then he grabs me by the upper arm and marches me toward the house. The crowd parts instinctively, and I notice all the Halloween costumes, the grotesque, the funny, the flashy, are like ghosts moving through my vision. It all feels unreal.

Maria is waiting by the front door with a younger version of Raphael and Salvador Costa. My chest tightens.

"It seems we have a problem," Papa says, frowning.

"Could we discuss this inside?" Maria asks cautiously.

"Yes, inside would be better," agrees the younger man, holding a hand to his chest. He turns to me. "I'm Gabriel Costa."

"Sophia," I say.

"I know," he replies with a smile. He ushers Maria and his father inside.

"Head for Antonio's office," I tell the group.

We move through the house, and I pull my arm free from Papa's grip to take the lead.

When we reach Antonio's office, I knock. The door swings open, and Raphael's eyes meet mine. Relief flashes across his face when we all step inside.

The office has always felt big to me, but tonight, it feels claustrophobic, as though the walls are pressing in, with so many men in the room.

Gabriel embraces Raphael. Raphael's hand goes to the back of Gabriel's neck in an affectionate hold.

"I'm so glad to see you," Raphael says quietly.

"And you, brother. When Maria used our code word, I feared the worst."

Salvador Costa leans forward, frowning. "What is going on?"

Papa glances at me, raising an eyebrow. "Why are you dressed like this, Sophia?"

Antonio steps to Raphael's side. "We think the Russians are trying to spark a war between us."

Papa chuckles, sliding into the chair behind Antonio's desk. "Did Sophia come up with this ruse to get out of marrying Raphael, or did Raphael decide my daughter isn't to his taste?"

"Neither," Antonio replies firmly.

Raphael pivots sharply, his eyes locking on his father. "Their security team at the back of the property... they're all dead."

Silence hits the room.

Papa straightens, shoulders stiff, eyes narrowing into razor slits. "Explain."

Raphael's voice drops, calm but hard, each word slicing through the tension in the room. "They were taken out before they could even react. Whoever did this is organized."

Salvador shifts on his feet, a flicker of unease crossing his face. "This... this isn't just a warning?"

"No," Antonio says, his hand resting lightly on Raphael's shoulder, a quiet show of control. "We think it's the beginning."

"Fuck," Papa hisses, the words sharp enough to cut. "Most of our guests are wearing masks. We'll never know who's friend or foe."

"Our men are not armed," Salvador states.

Behind me, Gabriel sucks his teeth and peels back his jacket, revealing a gun snug in its holster. "Some of us are."

"Gabriel!" Salvador snaps.

"Had we known this was a wedding and not

some bullshit Halloween party, we wouldn't be. But I thought it best to have a few armed in case it turned ugly... and it has."

Papa taps the desk, knuckles rattling on the polished wood. "But not with us, with the Russians. What do we do?"

Raphael tilts his head toward the basement. "You have enough guns down there to arm us all."

"And you know this how?" Papa asks, suspicion flashing across his features.

I raise my hand, and his frown deepens. "Raphael thought it best to keep us safe," I say, my voice steadier than I feel.

Raphael steps closer, sliding an arm around my shoulders. The contact is warm and firm. "Sophia said you taught her and Maria to shoot. It was a wise decision."

A part of me wants to pull away from him— this closeness feels dangerous—but another part can't help but be impressed he'd stand up to my father and back me openly.

Papa nods once, sharp and deliberate. "All my children can shoot." He glances at Salvador. "Can yours?"

Salvador tilts his head, a faint, cocky smile

tugging at his lips. "Unlike you, I only have boys. They can all handle a gun."

Raphael clears his throat. "We need to move discreetly, in groups. To keep everyone comfortable, groups of four. Two from your camp, two from yours."

Salvador raises an eyebrow at my father. Papa just nods, slow and deliberate.

"This will work for us," Papa says.

Raphael reaches for my hand. My pulse spikes, but I don't pull away. "It needs to look like the wedding is going ahead. You need to get dressed, Sophia."

"What?" My stomach knots.

"We need this meeting to look as though you had cold feet, but that it was resolved," he says, the edge of steel threading through his calm tone. "Your father goes out there and announces it. Let the guests know what's happening."

"As in… us getting married to merge the families?" I ask, my voice sharp, lined with steel.

Raphael's jaw tightens. "Exactly."

I swallow hard, my throat suddenly dry. The thought of standing at the altar, pretending this is all normal, makes my stomach twist into knots.

My eyes flick to Papa. He's already staring at me, like a predator assessing prey.

"And we're just... supposed to go along with this?" I ask, my hands curling into fists at my sides.

"You don't have a choice," Raphael says quietly. "Not if we want to survive the night."

I shiver, half from his nearness, half from the gravity of his words. Glancing around the room, my brother, Antonio, stands like a statue, his expression unreadable.

Papa leans back, exhaling slowly. "So, we do this quietly, efficiently, and without alarming anyone. Understood?"

"Yes," I say, though the word tastes bitter.

Raphael presses a hand to my lower back, guiding me toward the door. "Get dressed. Make it look like you're ready to walk down the aisle, but don't give anyone the satisfaction of thinking you're happy about it."

My stomach twists. I feel the weight of a hundred eyes on us, even though the room is empty. Every mask, every hidden glance, every whispered conversation outside is a potential threat. And yet, somehow, with him at my side, I feel a fraction of control, like maybe we can navigate this chaos without losing ourselves.

With one final glance at the men in the room, I grab Maria's hand, and we move out into the hall and up the stairs.

CHAPTER *Nine*

Raphael

Hector Chavez points at me, the motion slow and deliberate, like he's marking me for inspection. "You'll need to leave the guns in here." His hand rests on the doorknob of Antonio's office, fingers curling around the metal with a casual authority that makes my skin itch. "You, me, and your father will make the announcement. We'll all appear to be happy. Just one big happy family."

He opens the door, and the grin on his face is too wide, too sharp, like a predator showing teeth before the kill. "Let's do this."

Antonio and my brother, Gabriel, are going to

wait downstairs to arm our men. My father follows Hector out into the hallway. I give Gabriel a small nod, the kind that says *watch your back*, and then all of us leave the office.

The night hits me when we step outside. Cool air, sharp with the scent of fall and some metallic undertone—maybe tension, maybe fear. Torches flicker along the driveway, casting long shadows over the masked guests who chatter and murmur, oblivious to the undercurrent of danger threading through the crowd. I follow the leaders of both families, my eyes scanning every mask, every flicker of movement.

Hector climbs onto the ledge of a fountain in front of his house, shoes scraping against the stone. He raises a hand, waving theatrically at the partygoers. The murmur of the crowd rises, then falters as my father steps up beside him. The chatter dies almost instantly. Every guest knows something monumental is coming, even if they don't know what it is yet.

Hector clears his throat, voice booming, reverberating across the courtyard. "Tonight..." he begins, the words deliberate, measured, "... is not just a celebration of Halloween. It is a joining of families, of fortunes, and of futures. We stand together, united, stronger than we have ever been." His eyes sweep the crowd, resting briefly on faces hidden behind masks. "We've faced threats before, we've endured loss, but tonight we show the world that nothing can break us. Not rivalry, not violence, not betrayal. Tonight, we are one."

A ripple of forced applause spreads through the crowd. Masks turn slightly, curious eyes searching for any sign of weakness.

Salvador clears his throat. His tone is smooth, carrying a practiced weight. "Hector is right," he says, glancing briefly at me. "We are bound by more than tradition tonight. We are bound by the promise that our families will protect each other. That we will stand together in the face of *any* threat..." He pauses, letting the words settle like a stone dropped in a pond. "And let no one mistake this celebration for weakness. Power respects power, and tonight, we remind everyone who we are."

I glance at him, then at Hector, and finally back at the crowd. The tension hangs thick, almost tasting it on my tongue. Stepping slightly forward, I project my voice so the crowd can hear every word.

"We are stronger than any outsider who thinks they can divide us," I say. "And make no mistake, those who threaten our families will learn that loyalty and blood run deeper than fear. Tonight, we celebrate unity." I pause, letting my eyes sweep over the masks, the shadows flickering in the torchlight. "Tonight, Sophia Chavez and I *will* wed, and all of you *will* bear witness to the Chavez and Costa families becoming one."

A low murmur runs through the crowd. Masks shift, heads tilt, eyes flick behind painted smiles. Everyone's watching. Everyone's measuring.

Some clap—tentative, testing the air.

Others stare, frozen.

Downstairs, I know Antonio and Gabriel are waiting in the basement, ready to arm the men when they arrive. Upstairs, Sophia is behind closed doors, getting into her dress, preparing to play the part.

Hector clears his throat, voice rough and loud. "Tonight..." he says, "... we witness history! Two families, bound together by respect and loyalty." He grins at the crowd.

Salvador's eyes sweep the courtyard as he nods in agreement.

The crowd shifts again. Whispers spike like gunfire, slicing through the murmur.

Applause starts slow. A few clap at first, cautious, testing the ground. Then more join in, louder, filling the courtyard.

My father's hand lands on my shoulder. "To the Chavez and Costa families... may this be the first of many celebrations, and may this herald a legacy of peace."

The crowd erupts. Cheers, applause, raised glasses. Some nod at me, some smile behind their masks.

My father and Hector step down, shaking hands with a few of their closest allies, leaving me to move through a cluster of men loyal to my family. They crowd around me, slapping backs, gripping shoulders, offering congratulations with grins.

Carlo is the nearest. I've known him for a long time, long enough to trust him with my life.

"You kept this quiet," he says, grinning.

"There's another surprise for you," I reply, my voice low and sharp. "I want you and one other to go over to Hector Chavez. Offer him congratulations. Then I want you to take two of his men with you into the house and down into the basement."

Carlo steps back, frowning, brow furrowed. "Why?"

"No questions, my friend. Do it *now*," I order, letting my authority fill the space between us.

There's no room for hesitation.

Not tonight.

Not when the wrong move could get someone killed.

Carlo nods, taps the man behind him on the shoulder, and together they head toward Hector.

My father stands next to me. "Gentlemen, my son needs a moment to prepare for his bride. Give him some space. This will be one Halloween we're *never* going to forget."

Laughter and cheers ripple through the crowd as he guides me through it, through the masks and shadows, and into Hector Chavez's office.

The room is empty—surprisingly so.

"You understand why this has to happen?" he asks, eyes sharp.

"I do."

"You understand why you weren't brought in on the conversation?"

"I do not."

Dad's jaw tightens. "You've been obsessing over some woman you met last year. And I know you. Once you set your heart on something, no one can change your course. When Hector approached me with this idea, I knew, in the depths of my soul, that it was the right move for our family."

"You couldn't have explained it to me?"

He shakes his head slowly. "Sophia is beautiful. She'll make a fine bride."

I let the words settle, unspoken weight pressing in from all sides. "Yes," I say, low. "She will."

And I mean it.

CHAPTER
Ten

Sophia

Maria is doing up the countless tiny buttons on the back of my wedding dress. Each one feels impossibly delicate, like threading pearls through a needle. It's not a style I would have picked for myself. It's far too elaborate, frilly in a way that makes me feel like a porcelain doll. Clearly, my father must have chosen it. The fabric shimmers under the soft light of my bedside lamp, and I can't help but notice how stiff it feels around my shoulders, the way it pins me upright.

"This is not how I thought this day was going to go," I mutter, staring at my reflection in the full-length mirror. My hair is pinned up, perfect and tight, and I can see the tension in my neck and jaw reflected back at me.

"Me either," Maria says, her fingers working fast, agile, fumbling a little as she struggles with a particularly stubborn button. "I thought we'd sneak out at midnight, hit some of the local clubs. Never in a million years did I think you'd be getting married to someone you hardly know."

I trace the edges of the lace on my dress with a fingertip. "He seems nice, doesn't he?" I ask tentatively, trying to convince myself more than her.

"His reputation precedes him," Maria says, finally fastening the last button with a snap. "But he is infatuated with you. Maybe he'll make a good husband?" She shrugs, her voice a little teasing but not unkind.

I shift on the edge of the bed, feeling the fabric bunch uncomfortably at my hips. "What am I going to do?"

Maria sits beside me, close enough that her elbow brushes mine. "We'll figure it out." She tilts her head, a sly smile tugging at her lips. "I could accidentally shoot him tonight if things do get serious."

I laugh, surprised at how much relief bubbles up in the sound. I glance at her, locking eyes. "You'd do that for me?"

"Well..." she says, winking, "... I've only ever shot at targets. But I'd try. Just don't stand too close to him in case I miss."

I shake my head, grinning despite the tension knotting in my chest. Somehow, with Maria here, it feels like maybe I won't have to face this alone.

She tilts her head, eyes narrowing playfully as she studies me. "I have an idea. What if we did your makeup like the night you first met him? Your father won't like it, but it is Halloween after all."

"Defiant until the end. I like it." I stand and walk over to my dresser, the heels of my shoes clicking softly on the wooden floor. "Want me to do yours as well?"

"Yes, but make me look cute... to Gabriel." Her voice carries that familiar teasing lilt, but I catch the tiniest flicker of nerves beneath it.

"You're beautiful, honey, inside and out." I pull her into a hug.

Maria steps back, and I glance at her dress hanging in my closet, the soft, pale pink folds promising elegance and just a hint of mischief. "Go get dressed. I'll do my makeup first, then you."

Maria nods and does as she's told, and by the time she's finished, I have a white layer of makeup over my face.

Smiling at her, I say, "Day of the Dead, here we come."

CHAPTER Eleven

Raphael

Standing under the arch at the back of the Chavez estate, the autumn air is cool and carries the faint smell of smoke from the torches lining the pathway. My suit is tight, the jacket heavy on my shoulders, but I barely notice. My attention is elsewhere—on the arch, the decorations, the little touches I'm sure Hector Chavez insisted on. Pumpkins carved with grins too wide, cobwebs stretching between posts, black and orange ribbons fluttering in the wind. I can't help thinking it's a bit morbid having a Halloween-themed wedding arch. Maybe it's fitting, given

Sophia doesn't want this, and I've killed more people for my family and power than I care to think about. Or maybe it's a warning. Touched by death, all the time. Maybe this is the life I'm going into will be worse.

Gabriel is beside me, acting as my best man. His presence is solid, familiar, and steady. I glance at him. He's trying not to look nervous, but the twitch in his jaw tells me he is. I reach over and tap his shoulder. He nods, tightening his fists at his sides, in silent acknowledgment. He's worried, we all are, but so far, everything has been quiet.

The crowd is seated, a scattering of familiar faces and strangers alike, all waiting, all watching. The absence of the Russians is still heavy in my chest. My men, Antonio's men, everyone, have combed the property. The only anomaly was the Chavez family's dead security detail at the back gate, but even they were replaced quickly. Their bodies are gone, but the memory lingers. *Was this a test? A way to see if we could breach the Chavez estate without being caught?* If so, they failed. Every perimeter, every blind spot, every patrol accounted for. We are prepared.

I swallow, my throat tight, but I don't let it show. I won't. Not now. Not here.

A ripple of movement catches my attention. Maria appears at the end of the aisle, her heels clicking softly against the stone, her frame in the shadows of the torches. The wedding music starts, a slow, haunting melody that sets the pace of the day. My heart kicks in rhythm with it.

As she gets closer, she raises her face. The painted mask of Day of the Dead colors her skin in stark whites and blacks, reds and golds. It's beautiful. Morbid, like the arch. Like this wedding. Like this life. But still beautiful.

Then my eyes find her. *Sophia.*

Her father walks beside her, his hand firm on her elbow, his face unreadable, but I can see the anger as he escorts his only daughter, who is *not* dressed to his liking, I'm sure. A collective gasp goes through the crowd, but I don't pay attention to any of the guests. I only see her. And she looks like the day we met. Painted, defiant. Bold. Eyes holding mine.

I smile, a spark of hope igniting in my chest. I want her. Not just a wife who obeys, who submits, who follows. No. I want a partner. Someone who will fight, who will argue, who will challenge me every step of the way. And she will. I feel it in the tilt of her chin, in the fire in her eyes, and in her painted face.

She reaches the arch, her father stepping back, leaving her standing there like a queen of some dark kingdom. She is *mine*, and yet, she's unclaimed. Untouchable. Perfect in every imperfection.

The priest clears his throat. "We are gathered here today…" He pauses, glances at me, at Gabriel, then at Sophia. Standard wedding fare, but it falls flat against the tension in the air, against the pulse in my veins.

"Do you, Raphael, take Sophia to be your lawfully wedded wife?" His question hangs heavy in the night air.

"Yes," I say, voice low but firm. My eyes never leave hers.

"And do you, Sophia, take Raphael to be your lawfully wedded husband?"

Her voice comes steady, despite the crowd, despite everything. "Yes."

A breeze picks up, carrying with it the smell of

damp leaves, smoke, and candles. The torches flicker, shadows dancing across Sophia's face. Her painted mask makes her look...

Untouchable. Fierce. Dangerous.

I want that.

I want all of it.

The priest holds out the small, black velvet box with the rings. "These rings..." he says, his voice carrying across the quiet estate, "... are a symbol of your eternal love. As you exchange them, let everyone here witness the bond you are creating, a circle unbroken, unending, and true."

My eyes drop to the rings, then back to her. She takes the box in her hands, her fingers brushing mine, and I feel the tremor before I see it. Her hand shakes as she lifts my ring, eyes wide beneath the painted mask.

I reach for her hand, steadying her. "Hey," I murmur softly. "Take your time. You've got this."

She swallows, breath hitching, and I see the tension in her shoulders, the way her fingers clutch the ring. I slide my hand under hers, guiding her gently, until the ring slips perfectly onto my finger. Her grip lingers on mine, hesitant, and I offer a small, reassuring smile.

"See?" I whisper, voice low, almost private in the midst of all the eyes. "Perfect."

Her eyes meet mine, unmasked and defiant, and I nod, a spark of pride and something warmer, deeper, igniting in my chest. She smiles beneath the paint, and I can't help the small grin tugging at my lips.

Now it's my turn. I take the ring from the box, holding it between my thumb and forefinger. Her hand rises, slightly trembling, as I slide the band onto her finger. She catches her breath as I ease it over her knuckle, adjusting it until it fits snugly, perfectly. I press her hand gently in mine, letting her feel the reassurance in my grip.

"There," I murmur. "You're *mine* and I'm *yours*."

Her fingers curl slightly around mine, warm and strong despite the situation. I pull her hand to my chest, holding it there for a moment, and I know, without a doubt, that this is not just a promise of a day, a night, or a lifetime. This is a promise of fire, of partnership, of love unyielding.

"By the power vested in me..." the priest continues, "... I now pronounce you husband and wife."

Taking her hand in mine fully, I lift it slightly, feeling the weight of the moment. She leans into me, confident now, strong, and I know this isn't about submission. This is about partnership. About fire, trust, and two people choosing each other fiercely, against the world.

Taking a deep breath, I lower my forehead to hers, feeling the tension release just a fraction. A spark of laughter threatens to break free, and I fight it down, wanting to stay composed. But inside, I'm alive.

The priest nods toward me. "You may kiss the bride."

I glance down at her, seeing the faint flicker of hesitation in her eyes, the defiance that never fully leaves her. Smirking, I lean in slowly, giving her every chance to pull back, but she doesn't. She meets me halfway, lips brushing mine with a careful, deliberate pressure that makes my chest tighten.

The kiss deepens almost immediately, and I feel her respond, bold, unafraid, pulling me closer. Her hands find my shoulders, gripping just enough to let me know she's there by choice, not obligation. There's no faltering, no doubt—only fire and heat and the dangerous thrill of claiming each other fully, right here, right now, in front of all these people.

A murmur runs through the crowd, a mixture of shock and awe. Some of the older guests murmur about the audacity of it, about the painted mask and the boldness of the gesture. Others are smiling, clapping softly, caught up in the tension and release of the moment. My men shift slightly, alert but relaxed, eyes scanning, but knowing there's no threat right now—only us.

I pull back slightly, just enough to look into her eyes. They're wide, defiant, sparkling with something dangerous and alive.

"You've got quite a grip on me," I murmur, low, letting only her hear.

"I hope so," she replies, and the smirk she gives me beneath the paint makes my chest tighten again.

Glancing toward her father, who is still standing nearby, arms crossed, jaw tight. He looks like he's struggling to reconcile the defiance in his daughter with the weight of the moment. I nod slightly at him—not in arrogance, but in acknowledgment. She's his daughter, yes, but she's *mine* now, too, and she will always be her own woman.

The priest clears his throat again, and the applause breaks out. The guests are standing now, clapping, some even whistling, caught up in the drama and intensity of the kiss. Sophia laughs quietly into my chest, and I feel the spark of warmth, hope, and something unbreakable.

"Come on," I whisper, brushing a strand of hair from her face. "We've got a party to start."

She leans back slightly, still holding my hands, and nods, eyes bright. "Lead the way, husband."

We turn toward the reception, the music shifting, faster now, playfully teasing. Guests begin moving toward the tables, laughing and chatting. Maria dances by, clapping her hands, making sure everything is perfect, while my men take positions, alert but relaxed, eyes scanning the perimeter just in case.

I pull Sophia close, keeping her hand in mine, letting her feel the reassurance in my grip. She leans into me, her head resting lightly on my shoulder.

Leaning down, I press a quick kiss to her temple. "Ready?"

She lifts her head, eyes bright, smirk still in place. "Let's do this."

The reception is set just beyond the ceremony, tables lined with black linens and orange accents, candles flickering in carved pumpkins. The decorations are playful, morbid, and darkly beautiful.

We walk toward the tables, guests parting as we move through. My men and hers flank the sides, eyes sharp, scanning for threats. My focus is on her, the fire in her eyes, the way she carries herself as if she owns every step of this property.

The first dance is next, slow and deliberate. I pull her close, forehead resting against hers. The mask doesn't hide the heat in her eyes, the defiance that refuses to be tamed. I smile, letting myself imagine the life ahead, the battles we'll face, and the triumphs.

"This is ridiculous," she murmurs, voice low, but there's amusement in it. "We should be running, not dancing."

"Not yet," I murmur, brushing her hair back, ignoring the painted streaks that catch in my fingers. "Not yet. This is ours."

The music shifts, faster now, a playful note

underneath the haunting melody. Guests begin to smile, some even laugh. Maria flits between tables, helping here, laughing there, ensuring everything is perfect, as if she orchestrated not just the decorations but the courage it took to get Sophia here.

Sophia's father approaches, offering a nod, a grudging acknowledgment of the bond forming before his eyes.

"Congratulations to you both." He waggles a finger at Sophia and continues through the crowd.

"I like the makeup. It reminds me of the day we met."

"It feels like a lifetime ago," Sophia whispers.

"You liked me then."

Sophia smiles. "I still do. I just wish I'd had a choice."

"What if I make you a deal?"

Tilting her head to the side, Sophia's eyebrows come together in a frown. "What kind of deal?"

"Give me a year. If at the end of that year, you are truly not happy. I'll let you go."

Her eyebrows shoot up toward her hairline. "But our families would never agree to that."

I twirl her around on the dance floor, then bring her in closer. "Let me worry about that. What do you say, Princess? Can you give me a year?"

"Yes."

Our dance ends, and Maria rushes toward us. "If you look straight ahead, you'll see your cake." She grins at Sophia. "I'm pretty sure your dad has a weird sense of humor."

We both turn to stare at the wedding cake. It is morbidly elegant, black fondant adorned with sugar skulls, orange marigolds, and tiny edible pumpkins. Sophia smiles at it, wiggling her painted eyebrows, the mask only half hiding her amusement.

I lean close. "You like it?"

She smirks. "It's... appropriate."

Maria laughs. "It could be worse." She hands each of us a glass of champagne and disappears back into the crowd.

We clink our glasses together, the two of us untouched by the people around us. Guests dance, some awkwardly, some gracefully, some not at all. I notice the little things like the way she tilts her head when she laughs, how her eyes find mine even if she's only a step away.

I realize then that no matter how many enemies, how many threats, how many times the world will try to bend her or me, we will stand unbroken. Defiant. Together.

When the time comes for speeches, my men step forward first, offering words not just of loyalty but of belief in what we are building, in what we will always defend. Sophia's friends follow, laughter and stories threading together to form the tapestry of our life already beginning.

At one point, I catch her hand in mine, raising it just enough to brush my lips across her knuckles, a promise in a gesture. She doesn't pull away. She leans into it, letting me feel her warmth.

I glance across the property, taking notice of every corner, every shadow, every torch still burning.

The estate is secure.

My men are vigilant.

The night deepens. Candles flicker, pumpkins glow, shadows stretch long across the stone paths. We dance, we laugh, we toast, we celebrate. And I realize, quietly, that this is more than a wedding.

It's a declaration.

A challenge.

A start.

A promise.

The music swells again, a slower song this time, more intimate. I pull her close, our foreheads pressed together, and the world fades except for her, for us. A spark of hope ignites deep in my chest, burning brighter than any fear.

I whisper against her ear, "This is just the beginning."

"You've got one year, Raphael."

My heart skips a beat, and an ache forms in my chest. "Yes. But you have to try too."

"I will."

But there's a look in her eyes that says she's already looking for a way out.

Perhaps it was foolish of me to think we could make this work.

CHAPTER
Twelve

Sophia

Sitting alone in my childhood bedroom, the faint echo of the wedding fades. The house is quiet, almost reverent, and I trace the gold band on my finger absentmindedly. One year ago, I never imagined I'd be here, married to the man who set my world on fire—*literally*—then pulled me into something I didn't understand.

Raphael.

The Reaper.

The way he took over a room without speaking, in the way my body remembers him.

And then there is my father. The man who

should have protected me, but instead forced me into this marriage, this alliance between our families. All those carefully rehearsed smiles, the whisper of authority, the press of his hand at my elbow as he walked me down the aisle—it still stings. I realize, with a sinking weight, that maybe the dead security guards weren't the Russians after all. Maybe this was always meant to be a test of loyalty, a way to see if we could be contained, guided, controlled.

Shaking my head, I push away the memories, letting the present take over. I've changed into my going-away outfit. Pale pink. The same color as Maria's bridesmaid's dress. A flowing skirt swirls around my legs as I smooth the silk of my striped pink-and-white blouse. Matching shoes. My face is devoid of makeup except for my favorite lip gloss. I look comfortable, elegant, perfect for leaving a life I didn't ask to have and stepping into the one I choose with him.

Descending the staircase of my childhood home, and there he is. Waiting. *Raphael. The Reaper. My husband.* My body hums at the sight of him, the same magnetic pull I felt the first time he touched me, the same sharp, undeniable tension in the air whenever he's near. He smiles, just enough to make my heart skip a beat, just enough to remind me he knows exactly how to kiss me and make me melt, and just enough to make me trust him with the one-year promise he made.

One year to make or break us.

As I reach the second-to-last step, he extends his hand. The one with his wedding band glinting in the light. I let my hand slide into his, feeling the warmth, the strength, the promise behind the gesture. Together, we walk to the limousine waiting outside, my father's grand gesture of control, or perhaps ceremony. Raphael is calm, confident, the sort of man who commands presence without effort.

My father and Raphael's father are here, side by side. My father's eyes linger on me for a heartbeat longer than comfortable, but Raphael's father is all composure. Both of us kiss the cheeks of these men, the architects of our entwined lives, and I feel the weight of history pressing down, a silent acknowledgment that our lives are now bound in ways we can't undo.

Raphael opens the door for me, and I slide inside. The leather smells faintly of smoke and polish, warm and familiar in a dangerous way. I watch him shake hands with his brother before he slides in beside me. My pulse quickens, knowing it is just us now.

"Raise the privacy screen," he tells the chauffeur.

The partition lifts, and almost immediately, he pulls me onto his lap. His arms wrap around me, strong and unyielding, and his lips find mine in a kiss that makes everything else fade away. I melt into him slowly, every nerve on fire, every thought of Father, family, and betrayal slipping behind the wall of *his* strength.

He pulls back just enough to look into my eyes, breathing a little heavier than before. "I need to know something," he murmurs, voice low, intimate. "Are you… a virgin?"

I feel heat rise to my cheeks, embarrassment flooding through me. My heart hammers in my chest, but I nod, my voice catching even though I don't speak.

He smiles then, that slow, knowing smile that makes my knees weak. "It doesn't matter to me if you are or not," he says, pressing his forehead to mine briefly. "But I need to know, to make this easier for you tonight."

The honesty in his words, the care, the quiet dominance that makes me feel safe, it's intoxicating. He's pleased, I can see it, in the tilt of his jaw, the spark in his eyes. Pleased he will be my first, that he will guide me, that he will claim me fully.

I let out a shuddering breath, nestling against him, feeling the tension of the day, and the promise of what comes next settle into my bones.

One year.

One chance.

He kisses me again, softer this time, teasing, patient. His hands move, gentle but firm, exploring just enough to remind me that I am his. And I know, even with everything that's happened, that I'm excited to see where this will go.

Raphael is experienced. He knows how to touch me to make me gasp and melt, but when his fingers begin to pull down my underwear, I freeze.

"Trust me," he whispers between kisses.

"I don't want to do this in a car."

"We won't. But I want to taste you."

Scared and feeling out of control, I glance at the partition. "The driver?"

Raphael shakes his head as my panties slide down my legs. "He can't hear or see us."

He tilts his head, capturing my lips again, slower this time, deliberate, like he's mapping every inch of me with his mouth. My chest tightens, and a rush of warmth spreads through me—fire igniting from the tips of my fingers, down my arms, curling low in my stomach. I want to pull him closer, to feel more of him, but my mind fights to keep pace with my body, terrified of what 'more' could mean, yet craving it anyway.

His hands cradle my face, thumbs brushing my cheekbones, and I melt into the touch, lips parting instinctively. Every kiss teases, lingers, leaves me dizzy and disoriented. I feel the warmth of his body pressed against mine, the strength in his arms anchoring me even as desire coils tight inside me.

I want to lose myself in him, completely, but a part of me hesitates. A whisper of doubt, of fear, of the one-year promise he made.

Not a lifetime yet.

Not fully his.

My chest swells with longing, my knees weaken, and I let out a shuddering breath I can't control. He senses it. I can feel his smirk against my lips, the confidence that comes with knowing exactly the effect he has on me.

His tongue traces mine just enough to send sparks crawling up my spine, and my body responds instantly, hot, alive, aching for something I can't name. My hands clutch at his shoulders, gripping, seeking, wanting, yet my mind reels with the uncertainty of what 'more' might mean.

He pulls back slightly, resting his forehead against mine, just long enough for me to catch my breath, for the ache of wanting to twist through me.

His lips brush my ear as he murmurs, low, intoxicating, "You're already mine, Sophia. One year... we'll figure out the rest."

I can only nod, trembling slightly, warmth radiating through me, my pulse wild and unsteady. My body still burns and aches for more kisses, more contact, more of whatever it is he can give me, but the precise shape of it remains a delicious, frustrating mystery.

Every time his lips find mine again, I lose myself just a little more—wanting more, needing more, yet terrified of the surrender it implies. Raphael knows he's my first. I know he will guide me. And yet, I've never felt anything like this, and the pull is relentless, dizzying, overwhelming in the best way.

I gasp softly against him, a mix of shock and yearning, as my body continues to warm, ache, and melt under the pressure of his kisses. My mind can't name it, can't define it, but my body knows. It wants him. All of him.

And I'm terrified and desperate to see what comes next.

Raphael lays me gently across the back seat of the limousine, his movements slow, deliberate, never rushing me. The soft leather creaks beneath me as I shift. He shrugs off his jacket, tosses it aside, then pulls his shirt loose from his pants. The dim overhead light catches on the edge of his wedding band as his hands move.

My hands move before I think, sliding up under the material of his shirt. Heat radiates from his skin. My fingers trace the firm planes of his chest and back, feeling the tension coiled there like a live wire.

He leans down, undoing the first buttons of my blouse, his mouth brushing a trail of kisses between my breasts, lower, over my stomach. When he lifts my skirt, a jolt of fear and panic floods through me, sudden and overwhelming. My hands fly to his head, tangling in his hair, halting him.

His eyes flick up to mine instantly, dark and steady. "Relax, Princess."

"I don't... I don't want my first time to be in a car," I blurt out, voice trembling.

He stops completely, sitting back just enough to give me space. "I'm not going to fu—" He cuts himself off, jaw tightening, then softens. "I'm not going to make love to you in a car." His thumb strokes my hip gently. "But I want you to experience what it feels like before we have sex."

My heart thuds harder. "What... what feels like?" The words are barely a whisper.

Raphael's mouth curves into a slow, dangerous smile, but his eyes stay soft. He leans down again, pressing a kiss to my stomach, his breath warm on my skin. "Let me show you," he murmurs.

My pulse races. Part of me still trembles,

unsure, but another part—the part he lit on fire a year ago—wants to know. Wants to feel. Wants him.

Raphael pushes up the skirt and kisses the inside of my leg. Instinctively, I try to snap my legs closed. He pushes his face into me and breathes deeply, then his tongue strokes me. I jolt at the sensation, and he does it again.

"Let me taste you," he whispers.

Confused by the emotions and lust coursing through me, I stare at the ceiling of the car, not knowing what to do.

"Open your legs, Princess."

Embarrassed, I put an arm over my eyes and do as he says.

"Perfect," he whispers, and then I feel his mouth on me.

His tongue flicks over my nub, and instinctively, I spread my legs wider. This is no clumsy lover. Raphael sucks and flicks his tongue, and I find myself threading my fingers through his hair and holding him to me as I grind on his face. Abandoning all feeling of embarrassment, my body feels like it's reaching for something.

My thighs feel like they are on fire, then he

inserts his tongue inside me, and my body feels as though it's shattering. He sucks on my nub while wave after wave pulses through me. I scream his name as he keeps up his assault. It's only when every last tremor stops that he kisses his way up my body and lets me taste my own desire on his lips.

Panting, trying to steady my breathing, I feel Raphael's hands move with surprising gentleness as he fastens the buttons of my blouse again, one by one. His touch is warm, steady, almost protective now, and then he draws me into his arms.

"You're going to make a fine lover," he whispers against my hair.

A nervous laugh escapes me before I can stop it. "Will it... be like that all the time?" My voice sounds small, unsure, but there's a thread of curiosity laced through it that I can't hide.

Raphael chuckles softly, low in his chest. "No." He presses a kiss to the side of my face, lingering just long enough to calm the wild flutter of my heart. "Your first time won't be like that. But I promise you, as I learn your body, I'll do my best to make you feel good."

Something in his tone, which is steady, confident, and almost tender, settles the storm inside me. I still don't know what's coming, but with his arms around me and his breath warm against my skin, I start to believe he means it.

CHAPTER
Thirteen

Raphael

Sophia is curled into my side, her head resting against my shoulder as I watch the city fly by. The buildings blur past the tinted glass, lights smearing into streaks of gold and red. Three hours to the airport, then nine hours until Paris. Hector Chavez said she's always wanted to go there, so my father arranged it—one more move on the chessboard he's been playing with our lives. If it softens her heart toward me, maybe it's worth the trouble. If it doesn't, I'll find another way. I always do.

The chauffeur takes the same steady route

we've taken a dozen times through the city, past the old heart of Miami. The Miami City Cemetery rises on the left, with iron gates and low-slung mausoleums, palms leaning like sentries. I let my guard fall a fraction, the place looking like any other patch of the city. The ring on my finger glints where it can catch the light. Sophia has slipped into sleep somewhere between adrenaline and exhaustion. Even exhausted, she's trouble wrapped in a ribbon I'm determined to keep.

The limousine turns off the main road.

Not onto the service drive.

Not onto anything public.

The chauffeur steers inward, through the carved iron, onto a path between stones, slow but deliberate. For a beat, I think he's taking a shortcut, some odd mercy I didn't ask for. Then the trees close in and the path narrows, and I realize where the driver is taking us. The cemetery swallows the engine sound. Lamps throw long, twisted shadows.

It's wrong—all wrong.

I reach for the screen, the privacy divider between us and the outside, the little barrier that keeps the world at bay. It won't budge. Not a millimeter. My voice is too steady when I call the chauffeur's name, then louder, clipped. No answer. I try the intercom. Silent. I yank at the door handle. Stuck. Not jammed, the locking mechanism is engaged.

Panic is a flavor I don't like, but it sharpens me. I pull my phone, thumb the speed dial to my father. Call drops to voicemail. I call Antonio. No answer. My men, Hector's, the Chavez detail. I know where they should be, how fast they move. Running the numbers in my head, I realize they'll be an hour away at best.

We'll never make it.

The limousine slows and finally stops.

The engine's hum goes down to a purr. The doors unlatch with a soft mechanical sigh that sounds louder than it should in the quiet.

I look at Sophia. She's awake now, eyes wide.

"Stay," I tell her, bluntly, the word brokers no room for argument.

She shakes her head. "It's not safe," she says simply.

"It's safer in here." My jaw tightens. "Don't argue with me."

She shakes her head immediately as she slips her hand into mine. Her grip is firm, steady, defiant. The pale pink of her skirt flutters as she shifts closer, the silk blouse catching a line of light, stripes soft against the night. The matching shoes look delicate, but the set of her jaw says she won't be left behind.

I curse under my breath, knowing there's no changing her mind. With my free hand, I reach for the pistol hidden in a console that my chauffeur didn't know about. I check the magazine, then tuck it into the back of my pants beneath my jacket. The weight settles against my spine, a silent promise that whatever waits for us in the dark, I'll meet it head-on with her beside me.

I step out first, polished shoes on the gravel. Nothing at first but the hush of the cemetery, some distant city noise swallowed by the monuments. The air tastes like soil and old stone. I take another step, then turn back. Sophia is beside me, hand warm in mine, fearless or foolish or maybe both as we move together.

Someone flips the switch on a bank of lights, and hard, white beams slice through the dark. I didn't know you could make the dead stage their own theater, but suddenly the cemetery looks like an arena. From behind a tall, ornate tombstone, a man steps out, the cigar light throwing his face into a sickly orange. He moves like he owns every shadow he emerges from. For a second, I don't recognize him, but then he smiles at me, and I know it's Mikhail Orlov, head of the Russian mob here in Miami.

My chest tightens.

My men are an hour away.

The edge of the night presses in.

I don't like numbers that don't end in our favor.

He smiles, the cigar burning low, and it's a gesture that says he expects the script. He takes his time, savoring the moment like he's about to ruin someone's life for the pleasure of it. This is the sort of man who thinks fear is a flavor to be sampled slowly.

I move before I think, because moving is what I do. So I step forward, tightening my hand on Sophia's. My voice is already low, controlled. "Back up," I say to him. "You don't want this."

He laughs, a dry sound, and the laugh spreads through the little ring of men emerging from behind stones—figures who know how to raise a cemetery into a battleground. They fan out, silhouettes between mausoleums, slow and deliberate. My gaze flicks to Sophia because she's mine and because she's the only thing in this place that matters the way air matters.

She surprises me.

Slipping her hand from mine, she lifts a gun I didn't even know she had, holding it like it's a natural extension of herself. The motion is fluid, practiced, nothing like the sheltered girl she was supposed to be. In a heartbeat, the weapon comes up to shoulder height—and she fires.

The sound cracks through the graveyard, sharp as a command, and my breath catches. The shot is clean, strong, and it throws the nearest man's shoulder back. Sophia doesn't hesitate. She tugs at my arm, and we move, ducking between headstones, stone biting our shins, the world suddenly a maze of monuments and shadow and the smell of cigar, smoke, and iron.

Her words come out like a grenade and hit me clean in the chest. "Nuh-uh," she spits, pulling me deeper into the graves, her voice steady in a place made for silence. "I'm not dying a virgin. You are going to make love to me, give me more orgasms, and the best year of my life, Raphael Costa, and maybe, just maybe, we'll survive a year together. Until then, take my gun and kill as many sons of bitches as you can."

She fires again, and the bullet's kiss takes a man down.

Adrenaline slams into me hard enough to make my vision narrow to her. *My Sophia.*

A grin spreads across my face, quick and feral, catching me off guard. Her hand fits into mine as I take the gun, a second piece of steel warming my palm. Force meets force—that's who I am, that's how I fight. The first shot cracks out clean, aimed where it counts, then another, and another. We move as one, me covering, clearing bodies from our path, and cutting their numbers down.

Sophia is ridiculous, brave, and utterly perfect.

We duck behind a ridge between two monuments, stone cold against my back. I steal a quick kiss against the side of her face. Bullets scream past us, striking marble and granite, ricocheting off headstones with sharp, metallic whines. Shards of stone spit into the air, the cemetery itself becoming part of the fight. I lean out, squeeze the trigger, and send rounds snapping back. Men scatter near the largest tomb, the formation breaking as my shots land, while the night erupts with ugly, decisive violence.

At a lull, I press my forehead to hers, both of us panting.

"You really are my dream come true, Sophia Costa," I tell her, because if there's one thing I'm sure of in the middle of all this, it's *her*.

Cupping her cheek with the hand that still wears the ring that binds us for now, a ring that means nothing against the math of bullets but everything for the ledger of my heart.

She elbows me. "Then act like it. Get us the fuck out of here."

Her challenge burns in my blood, and the grin comes easy. Let the dead keep their silence.

Graveyard promises aren't broken. They are survived.

We push forward, two shadows slipping between graves, guns ready, lungs burning, hearts pounding. Beyond the stone and silence, the city keeps humming, blind to the war in its cemetery. Sophia Costa won't go quietly, and this man sure as hell doesn't back down.

We move forward, two shadows gliding between headstones, lungs burning, hearts thundering.

From the far side of a crypt, his voice drifts out, thick, heavy, every word rolled in that deep Russian growl. *"Costa... you cannot run forever. The girl will not save you."* The accent drags on the vowels, hardens the consonants. The sound rakes over my nerves, cold as the marble at my back.

Sophia and I stay low, silent, slipping from one patch of shadow to the next. The dead don't complain about our trespass, but the living hunt us with intent.

Up ahead, through a row of crumbling headstones, I spot a gap in the fence—*a way out.* I catch her wrist, point toward it, then motion for her to go. Her face turns to me, defiance blazing even in the dark. Sophia shakes her head hard.

No.

Leaning closer, my breath brushes her ear. "Go. I'll be right behind you... as soon as it's safe."

Her eyes lock on mine, wide, full of fire and hesitation. Indecision clouds her face for a split second before she grabs my jacket, pulls me in, and crushes her mouth to mine. The kiss is fierce, desperate, hungry like a woman staking her claim in the middle of hell.

When she pulls back, her voice is ragged but steady. "You'd better be right behind me."

Her words cut sharper than any bullet. And God help me, I'll bleed this cemetery dry before I break that promise.

Sophia crouches low, skirts brushing damp grass, and she slips through the jagged break in the fence. My chest tightens as I watch her vanish into the dark beyond the headstones. Then she's clear, darting across the cracked asphalt of the service road, fast, determined, every step pounding like a drumbeat in my head.

The shot comes sharp, splitting the night.

Time slows.

I see her body jerk mid-stride, the force lifting her clean off her feet. She sails through the air, a twisted arc against the streetlight glow, before crashing down hard onto the pavement.

My throat locks.

She doesn't move. Not an inch. Just a small, broken shape on the ground, the fire in her snuffed out in an instant.

Rage boils through me, thick and hot. The

world narrows to the echo of that gunshot and the sight of Sophia crumpled on the road.

The shot still echoes in my ears when I spot the bastard who pulled the trigger. Rage steadies my hands. I stand tall, lift the gun, and line up the sight. One squeeze, one bullet, and his skull snaps back in a spray of red. He's dead before the bastard hits the ground.

The satisfaction lasts half a heartbeat. Then the night erupts. Gunfire rains down, bullets smashing into stone around me, ricochets whining off headstones, shards of marble exploding into the air like shrapnel. I drop, covering my head with one arm, teeth clenched against the storm. Dust chokes the air, acrid and heavy.

When the barrage eases, I dare a glance toward the asphalt. My heart freezes. The spot where Sophia's body lay is empty.

Gone.

For a beat, I can't breathe, and then hope punches through my chest, raw and savage.

She's alive.

She has to be.

I bolt, sprinting low and fast for the gap in the

fence, every muscle burning with the need to reach her. If she's out there, if she's breathing, then nothing in this graveyard or the next will keep me from her.

CHAPTER
Fourteen

Sophia

Biscayne Park looms ahead, trees crowding together, the night thick with damp earth and the hum of crickets. I press my back to a trunk, bark rough against my skin, one hand clamped over my shoulder. The wound burns hot, a pulse of fire with every breath. It hurts like a bitch, but I'm alive.

If I can make it across the park, to the lights and noise of the streets beyond, maybe I'll survive. *Maybe we both will.*

Then the night erupts—gunfire, rapid and relentless, tearing through the quiet. I freeze, pressing myself tighter against the tree, heart surging. Footsteps follow, pounding the dirt. Someone's running.

I hold my breath. *Please, not them. Please—*

Raphael streaks past me, a shadow in motion. Relief bursts in my chest, sharp and overwhelming. "Raphael," I whisper, soft but desperate.

He stops dead, pivots, then rushes back to me. The next second, I'm crushed against him, his arms locking me in, fierce and unyielding. Pain rips through me, and I bite down hard on my lip to keep from screaming in agony.

He pulls back, holding me at arm's length, and his eyes drop to my blouse. Pale pink and white silk, ruined now, the shoulder drenched in a dark, spreading stain. His jaw tightens, fury flashing in his gaze.

I shake my head quickly. "We have to keep going. We need to get to the other side of the park."

He doesn't argue, not yet. Instead, he crouches slightly, inspecting the wound, his fingers surprisingly gentle as they press around the torn fabric. His eyes flick back to mine, hard and searching. "Can you run, Princess?"

If I speak, he'll hear the hesitation, so I just nod. Raphael's hand presses firmly against the small of my back. I kick off my shoes, the grass cold under my feet, and we take off, darting through trees and open stretches, lungs burning, hearts pounding. We don't stop until the chain-link fence looms ahead, the only thing between us and the street beyond.

Raphael grips the fence and scales it like it's nothing, every movement smooth, powerful, controlled. Even in the dark, even in the chaos, I can't help noticing how damn agile he is, how strong. He swings over the top, lands light on his feet, and looks back at me.

I grab the chain-link, metal biting into my palms. My shoulder screams the second I haul myself up, pain white-hot and blinding. For a heartbeat, I want to stop, but I grind my teeth, shove the fear down, and keep climbing. Determination is the only thing I have left.

At the top, my grip falters.

The world tilts.

My body pitches forward—falling.

Strong arms catch me before the ground can.

Raphael pulls me tight against his chest, lowering me carefully but not letting go. My breath hitches, pain clawing through me, but his hold is steady, unshakable.

Raphael's arms lock around me as if I weigh nothing. The world sways, the rhythm of his stride pounding against the chaos still echoing in the cemetery behind us. My head lolls against his chest, the scent of sweat and gunpowder clinging to him, the steady thud of his heart in my ear.

Pain claws through my shoulder, sharp and unrelenting, dragging the edges of my vision into darkness. I try to fight it, try to hold on, but my body betrays me.

The last thing I feel is the strength of his grip and the sound of his breath before everything slips away.

CHAPTER Fifteen

Raphael

Headlights cut through the dark, a horn blares, and a car skids to a screaming halt just feet from where I stand with Sophia in my arms. Tires burn rubber, smoke curling in the air.

Sprinting to the passenger side, I yank the door open and lower her into the seat like she's made of glass. My hands linger, brushing the blood-matted silk of her blouse, then I slam the door shut.

No time.

Vaulting onto the hood, I slide across the hood and rip open the driver's door. The man behind the wheel barely gets a word out before I drag him into the street, dump him on the asphalt, and swing myself into the car.

The engine growls, tires scream, and I put the city behind us, one red light at a time. Sophia's head lolls against the seat, every bump stealing another piece of my sanity. The hospital lights finally blaze ahead, salvation wrapped in white brick and neon.

I'm out of the car before it's even stopped, cradling her against my chest as I charge through the doors. "Help!" My voice is raw, stripped bare.

The medical team swarms, voices overlapping, hands reaching. They rip her from me, lay her on a gurney, and push it through the double doors. A nurse shouts at me, words I don't hear. My eyes are locked on Sophia as they tear open her shirt, the wound glaring back at me, red and ugly.

The nurse plants both hands on my chest, shoving me back, but I don't move. She pushes harder, then freezes when her eyes drop to the gun still clutched in my fist.

Her face drains of color.

She backs up.

Security floods in, black uniforms, heavy boots,

forming a wall around me. Someone grabs my wrist, twists, and the weight of the gun slides from my hand. Only then do I blink, drag my gaze from Sophia to the nurse.

My voice cracks as the words fall out, bare and true. "Please… make sure she's okay. I'm not sure what I'll do without her. She's *mine*. She's my wife."

Adrenaline locks my jaw into a hard line. Instincts take over before grief can calcify.

"Lock this place down," I tell the nearest guard, voice low and cold. "Keep everyone out. No one in, no one out."

He hesitates, then moves, barking commands, moving into action.

"This is war," I tell them, loud enough for more than the nearest to hear. "The Russians declared it the second they fired. Sophia's the first casualty." The words land like a blow. Heads turn. Conversations stop.

A hand lands on my forearm, soft and urgent. The nurse, her face a mask of professional calm, says, "Sir, you've been shot."

My gaze drops. A dark line along my bicep, warm under the fabric. Fingers find it, test the skin. Muscles contract on command.

"No," comes out flat. "Just a graze." The lie tastes like steel, but it steadies me.

A security guard fills the space between me and the door, blocking the exit like he owns the line. He's square-shouldered, committed. The thought of being held here spins the room.

No.

"Listen," I say, slowly and dangerously. "I am Raphael 'The Reaper' Costa. Do not try to stop me, or you'll feel my wrath." My voice doesn't need to rise because the name gives it all the weight it needs. Pointing at Sophia, I say, "Keep her safe. Do whatever you need to do. I will pay you handsomely."

Contracts and threats—one for protection, one for obedience. The guard's jaw tightens, the choice grinding behind his eyes. He steps back. The line holds.

Gabriel is waiting at the doors, his face a map of concern. No questions, only a look, a nod.

Outside, the car I stole still idles. Sliding in, I put it in drive, and Gabriel climbs in beside me. "Alert the men," I order without looking. "Tell Antonio and Hector. Tell the Chavezes. Head for

Miami Cemetery. Orlov's men started this, and unfinished business ends tonight."

Gabriel's reply is already in motion as his thumbs fly over his phone. Tires spin, and we disappear into the city, every red light a countdown and every block a pulse closer to the place where graves and promises collide.

We park a little way down the road, out of sight of the iron gates. Gabriel and I climb out, shoes hitting asphalt. A handful of our men melt out of the shadows with their faces set, rifles slung, eyes on the cemetery. Carlo is there, grin gone, offering an Uzi with the businesslike calm of a man who's never surprised by blood. The metal is cold in my hands, but the weight feels right.

"No speeches," Gabriel says, voice flat. "Sweep, clear, move."

We slip through the gap in the fence, ghosts among stones. Headstones throw long black bars across the ground, where the tombs hide more than grief tonight. Men step from the shadows like they were carved there—Orlov's boys, scattered, searching for me. Thinking I'm hiding, but I'm not, not anymore. Targets are taken down fast, hard, and efficiently. No time for hesitation. Shots crack, ricochet bites at marble, silhouettes fall and stop moving. Men who try to fight are ended where they stand, and others drop their weapons and curl up, hands over heads, but hope dies quickly in the dark.

Carlo moves like a machine, Uzi barking in short, controlled bursts. Gabriel covers our flank, measured and merciless. The plan is simple— find them, make them pay, and take the ground back. We push deeper where lanes of graves become a maze of cover and shadow. Every nook gets checked, and every tomb is a room to clear.

No sign of Mikhail Orlov. Not behind the big family crypts, not in the mausoleum rows, not in the low tangles by the service road. Men fall around us. By the time the firing thins to occasional pops and the immediate threat has been shredded, the cemetery is littered with bodies, but Mikhail isn't one of them.

The quiet after is sharp.

We tally, breathe, reload.

Carlo's face is stony.

Gabriel curses under his breath and looks at me. "He slipped," he says. "Either out or deeper in."

"Or he left when the first shot rang out," comes the harder answer in my head. Either way, the message was sent. Orlov's men learned tonight what it means to try and touch what's ours.

We withdraw in formation, bodies left where they fell, the dead tell no tales. The fence creaks as we climb back out. The night swallows our footprints. No Mikhail. No closure. Only the cold, returning weight of what we'll do next.

"Find Mikhail Orlov," I tell the men, my voice flat and cold. "Any of his boys… bring them down. Don't come back without him or a body."

Carlo hesitates, grips tight on the Uzi. "Boss, where are you going? Don't you want to be in on the sweep? This is our chance to overthrow the Russian scum once and for all."

A hard laugh escapes, more sound than humor. "My place is with my bride." The words land like a verdict. "If she doesn't make it, neither will this peace between the families. Everything we built… gone. I won't trade her for a victory."

Men peel out into the dark again, they will comb the streets, alleys, every place Orlov's dogs might have run. Carlo gives one last look, unreadable, then moves. Gabriel falls into step beside him, phones already working, alerting eyes and ears across the city.

Engine still warm, the city lights blur into streaks as the hospital sign grows bigger. A guard meets me at the door, face all business and tired eyes.

"No one got near her," he says flatly. "She's in the ICU. Can I take you up?"

"Yeah." The word comes out like a held breath finally released. "Thank you. For keeping her safe. How many of you?"

"Twenty." The answer is clipped.

"Good." Comes the promise before anything softer finds me. "You'll be paid. All of you."

The guard's jaw tightens, and a nod is the only thanks he offers. No theatrics. Just duty.

The elevator smells of metal and antiseptic. The guard presses the button for the ICU floor. The doors open, and he escorts me past nurses and doctors who look up and then away.

A chair sits by her bed. Somehow, Sophia looks

smaller with the hospital lines and tubes. She is pale, but breathing steadily. My hand finds hers. She feels warm, stubborn, and more real than anything else in the room.

I curl her fingers around mine. No swagger left. No threats. Just a promise held between knuckles and skin as monitors beep, and the city hums beyond the windows.

I sit, shoes heavy on the linoleum, and hold on. Her eyelids flutter, while a shred of a smile ghosts her lips in sleep.

The men are out hunting ghosts and names.

For now, the only war that matters is the slow fight for the woman sleeping in this stark room. My hands closed around hers, a promise sharp in my chest, as I keep vigil.

CHAPTER
Sixteen

Sophia

Two Months Later

The first thing I see is the Eiffel Tower, a dark silhouette against a pale Paris morning through the hotel window. A smile slides across my face before a cheeky kiss lands right on my butt. I roll over, and the grin grows. Raphael is a map of temptation, planting kisses up my side, over my ribs, pausing to press one to my lips. Warm, stubborn, claiming.

My shoulder nags—an ache that's lived with me since the cemetery—but it's not the sharp, white-hot terror it once was. The bullet went clean through. The surgeon said it missed bone and arteries. Lucky, she called it. Lucky, stubborn, and a pain in the ass.

From what the doctors told me, and what I've lived through these last two months, healing isn't tidy. The skin closed up fast enough—stitches came out, the scar puckered into a pale line—but the muscle underneath took its sweet time learning to behave again. Physio became a thing that eats parts of the day, with small, stupid exercises that feel useless in the moment but add up to being able to raise my arm without a hot spike of pain. Cold mornings still make the shoulder grumble. Sudden movements are a reminder that I need to take it easy.

Recovery came with its own griefs and small victories. Coming here to Paris was a defiant, ridiculous, perfect choice. Proof that life could move forward. First steps down the hotel stairs with the sling were clumsy and brave. The first time I reached for a coffee cup with my right hand and didn't wince was a victory.

The surgeon's cautionary phrases of *'take it easy,' 'don't overdo it,'* hung around like an annoyed aunt, but Raphael's impatience with caution made me laugh more than once. He wants action—the doctors want caution. Somehow, we meet in the middle with gentle hands and dangerous promises.

Raphael's been more surgery-cleaning and stubborn-care than I expected. Small rituals started with helping to strap on physio bandages, pressing warm towels to the knot of muscle under the wound, and kissing the place where the scar is paling until it aches in a good way. There's a feral pride in watching him care for me.

He's protective and ridiculously tender, lifting me off a curb or putting his coat over my shoulder when the wind bites.

The first week, he kept me close as though I were something rare. The second month, he started pushing me harder by encouraging me to reach, stretch, and test the limits. He wasn't cruel, just relentless in the way men who love can be.

Raphael pulls my body gently toward him, lips finding the curve of my shoulder where the scar is, then moves to my mouth. The ache in my shoulder flares, then fades under the press of him. It's not only my body that's mending, it's the past two months that have been a messy stitching of trust, trial, laughter, and small, private vows. Paris is loud with possibility. The one-year clock still ticks, but for the first time in a long time, it sounds less like a countdown and more like a beginning.

He leans back a fraction, his forehead resting against mine, and asks quietly, "How are you feeling?"

The question pulls together all the small aches and the big stuff—the scar, the nights, the flash of the cemetery—and I answer honestly. "Tired. Sore. Lucky."

His thumb sketches circles along the hollow of my jaw. "Lucky," he repeats. He studies my face until the room shrinks to the two of us. Then the words come, low, plain, and everything, "You mean more to me than anything. I love you, Sophia."

The sentence lands, and the air shifts. Letting it sit feels dangerous and impossible at once. My heart fights its cage for a second, and then slow awareness spreads through me—this man who broke me open is the same one who's been putting me back together. A soft laugh bubbles up, half disbelief, half relief.

My hand moves and my fingers cup his face—soft palm to stubbled cheek—bringing him closer. The kiss is soft at first, honest, and when I whisper it back against his mouth, it feels like staking my claim in return.

"I love you too," I tell him, and the words are small, steady, and finally mine.

He smiles down at me, slow and dangerous in the way that makes my knees go soft. Then his mouth is everywhere, soft kisses along my jaw, a trail over my cheek, a ridiculous, tender assault that makes me giggle out loud. The sound is small and bright in the room. He pulls back and studies me, like he's memorizing each freckle and scar.

"Mikhail?" I blurt before I can stop myself, because the thought has been gnawing at the edges of everything since the cemetery. "Did you... did you find him?"

Raphael's face tightens for the fraction of a breath it takes to answer, "We ran their boys out of Miami," he says, his voice even. "But they'll be back. They always come back." He reaches for my hand and folds our fingers together. "Mikhail Orlov isn't dead. No trace. We think he went home to Mother Russia. For now, he's a ghost in the wind. We keep looking. We will always look."

A silence settles between us, not empty so much as full of plans.

"What about us?" I ask finally because there's a future to be carved out of this mess, and I want to know where I fit in it.

"Together we will rule the families. You're going to get a crash course in what we do, Princess," he says, like the words are a promise and a challenge all at once. "Your father will hate it. He wanted you barefoot and pregnant within a year. This upends that. It will rile him more than anything." His thumb traces the scar on my shoulder where the bullet slipped through. "But there's no one I trust more with my heart, or my empire, than you."

Heat floods me at the weight of his words. *Empire. Heart.* Not empty phrases from a man who knows how to use words as weapons.

Raphael leans in, voice low, almost a growl made soft by the smile in it. "Graveyard promises," he murmurs, pressing his forehead to mine. "We made them in blood and stone. We'll keep them... together."

The word settles there, heavy and real, and for

the first time since the cemetery, I believe it might be true.

THE END

Hey there, lovely reader!
Thanks a million for grabbing this book –
you rock!
Now, I'm not above a little shameless begging…
Pretty please, with a cherry on top,
leave a review wherever you picked this up.
Your thoughts help other readers discover my
wild and wonderful world of romance
and mayhem.
Plus, you'll earn major karma points!
Thank you for supporting indie authors like me.
Stay awesome!

The Savage Angels MC Series

Savage Stalker Book 1
The Savage Angels MC Series

BLURB

Dane Reynolds

President of the Savage Angels MC.
Fierce, strong, and loyal.
He's had his eye on Kat for a while now and has
been waiting for her to come to him, but he's had
enough of waiting.
He's decided it's time to make her his.

Kathleen Kelly

Katarina Saunders

Kat to the world, international rock star.
Lead singer for The Grinders.
Until she has an accident that ruins her career and
sends her running into the mountains, away from
everything and everyone.
Will these two come together?

Or will Kat's *savage stalker* get to her first?

**From *USA Today* Bestselling Author
Kathleen Kelly.**

Savage Fire Book 2
Savage Town Book 3
Savage Lover Book 4
Savage Sacrifice Book 5
Savage Rebel (Novella) Book 6
Savage Lies Book 7
Savage Life Book 8
Savage Christmas (Novella) Book 9
Savage Release Book 10
Savage Heart Book 11
Savage Angels Book 12
Savage Angels MC Collection Books 1-9

OTHER BOOKS
To Enjoy
by Kathleen Kelly

The MacKenny Brothers Series
An MC/Band of Brothers Romance

Spark Book 1
Spark of Vengeance Book 2
Spark of Hope Book 3
Spark of Deception Book 4
Spark of Time Book 5
Spark of Redemption Book 6
Spark of Passion Book 7

The Tackling Series
A Sports Romance

Tackling Love Book 1
Tackling Life Book 2

Wraith Novels

Wraith

Fealty: A Wraith Novel

Wraith Boxset

(Includes: Wraith, Fealty, and Shadow,
which are only available in this box set.)

Standalones

Cardinal: The Affinity Chronicles Book 1

Snake's Revenge: Gritty Devils MC

The Secrets We Hold

Check these links for more from
Kathleen Kelly

READER GROUP

Want access to fun, prizes and sneak peeks?
Join my Facebook Reader Group.
https://bit.ly/32X17pv

NEWSLETTER

Want to see what's next?
Sign up for my Newsletter.
https://www.subscribepage.com/kathleenkellyauthor

BOOKBUB

Connect with me on Bookbub.
https://www.bookbub.com/authors/kathleen-kelly

GOODREADS

Add my books to your TBR list
on my Goodreads profile.
http://bit.ly/1xsOGxk

AMAZON

Buy my books from my Amazon profile.
https://amzn.to/2JCUT6q

WEBSITE

https://kathleenkellyauthor.com/

TWITTER

https://twitter.com/kkellyauthor

INSTAGRAM

https://instagram.com/kathleenkellyauthor

EMAIL

kathleenkellyauthor@gmail.com

FACEBOOK

https://bit.ly/36jlaQV

ABOUT THE
Author

Kathleen Kelly, a USA Today Best-Selling Author originally from Penrith, NSW, Australia, now happily resides in Toowoomba, Queensland with her childhood sweetheart and their fur baby, Freya.

When not writing steamy romance novels with a HEA (for now) :), Kathleen can be spotted in local cafes, blending in with the regulars while plotting her next tale of passion and intrigue.

She finds inspiration in the quirky characters around her, real and fictional alike.
Kathleen welcomes messages from readers who share her love for stories that leave hearts racing and cheeks blushing.

If you have any questions about her novels or would like to ask Kathleen a question, she can be contacted via e-mail:

kathleenkellyauthor@gmail.com

or she can be found on Facebook. She loves to be contacted by those who love her books.